Alicia Cahalane Lewis

ROOM SERVICE PLEASE

ALICIA CAHALANE LEWIS is a ninth generation Quaker from the Shenandoah Valley of Virginia. She holds an MFA in creative writing from Naropa University where her poetry appeared in *Not Enough Night.* Her chapbook, *The Fish Turned the Waters Over So The Birds Would Have A Sky*, a contemplative meditation on the origins of evolution, was published by The Lune Chapbook Series. She is the author of *The Intrepid Meditator*, the recently published companion book to *Room Service Please*. Alicia continues to live and work in the Shenandoah Valley providing individual and group meditation classes in alignment with Reiki methods.

aliciacahalanelewis.com

ROOM SERVICE PLEASE

Room Service Please

Alicia Cahalane Lewis

Tattered Script Publishing

Tattered Script Publishing
PO Box 1704
Middleburg, Virginia 20117
tatteredscript.com

ISBN 9781737521938
ISBN 9781737521921
Printed in the United States of America
10 9 8 7 6 5 4 3 2 1

Tattered Script Publishing: Crafting Cultural Creativity and Authenticity

Cover art by J. Felice Boucher
Cover design by Emily Kallick

First Printing, 2022

While the names of the famous ballroom dancer Irene Castle, the 1920's Hollywood starlet Agnes Ayres, and the Waldorf-Astoria Hotel manager Lucius Boomer appear here, as do some "Social Notes" entries from The New York Times, June 18-21, 1922, *Room Service Please* is a work of fiction in its entirety.

For my daughter, Lydia, with love

Contents

Prologue

Sometime in that moment when life takes your hand and ushers you through a door, the door revolves, your hand gets pulled, and you step eagerly into an unknown. I won't say that this motion is an easy one, but one to behold for it happens to us all. We go through this door ushered in by only our absurd sense of self, our darn attitude, and our attempt at something reasonable, yet uncertain.

This was the way things were on the night of my sixteenth birthday. I never saw the door opening. I might have at one time seen only its closing, but once I stepped through that revolving door and into the Waldorf-Astoria Hotel foyer, I saw only opportunity. I was led from one realm and into another, and unbeknownst to me, ushered through one happy accident after another. Of course I knew nothing about hotels or foyers or steps that would take me across one room and into another. I knew nothing about men. I had only an idea of what they should be: attentive, passionate, eager.

Such naiveté. I use these words now, six years later, and laugh. Men are none of these things as they are all of them. They are absurd creatures I have come to appreciate. They are not easy to understand, but that is on me. I must continue to turn, to revolve, to look past obstacles that once stood before me and walk through new doors. I am a dancer. I dance. I feel certain that I will dance my way through this life easily putting one foot in front of the other, but I was not always this way. Where once I stumbled, I can now say I understand what it takes to high-step one's way through closed doors and accept the inevitable. Life is what we take, but more than that, life is what we are shown. It is on us to accept this. Or not.

I

June 18, 1922

Sunday mornings in New York City are placid. The night slips easily away to that rush of morning chill when inattentive minds awake slowly. There is motion in the street, but there is nothing to discern about the noise. These are the sounds one becomes accustomed to. They are nothing special. Nothing worth telling. Nothing. Does nothing have a sound? And if you were to describe nothing what words would you use?

Nothing should be black space. Emptiness. Regret. These words are necessary when describing the sound of nothing. But because my nothing once bore into me the way metal grinds on asphalt, my nothing was trolley wheels on a battered, slipshod rail. The shout of one lonely woman into the vestibule of the Waldorf-Astoria Hotel and the echo of her own voice returning to her. I couldn't understand what she was saying, but because there was nothing worth knowing about her, I turned to look out the hotel window just to be sure that nothing had not been superseded by something.

I had nowhere to go. I could have returned home, but that required taxi fare I did not have. My party shoes were soiled, my legs tired from dancing, and I did not have a penny to my name to call my ma. There was nothing to do but wait. I would wait until the empty street began to fill again or some bigger nothing swallowed me whole.

I hadn't a care in the world. Or did I? You will want to know why I was in the Waldorf-Astoria Hotel in the wee hours of the morning. I should tell you that turning sixteen is complicated. Or perhaps you already know? You will know what I know. Feel what I once felt, grumbling and complaining in all the right places to let your ma know just how miserable your life really is. But then what? You turn sixteen, in a confectionary, on a dance floor, in a hotel foyer, in a gentleman's room. With a chaperone or without one. Let me think just how I will share with you what might have been the most unrehearsed night of my life.

<>

It was on the eve of my sixteenth birthday when, against all reason, Ma bought me a pair of head-turning party shoes. She pulled at a snag in her limp stocking, took a long look at me in those caramel-colored heeled slippers, ostentatiously adorned with large satin bows, and threw away caution. I saw the wheels in her mind turn the way a worn handle turns on a meat grinder pushing blood into a vice. She was once young, I reasoned, wanting something like a pair of new shoes. Hadn't she told me all those stories of Jersey City, and want? I didn't grow up to put my head down and walk in shoes not destined for me, I told her, but my ma, my God-has-plans-for-us ma, will always see the world differently.

Ma took the money she was saving for someone, God, I guess, and pushed those hard-earned pennies across a dime-store counter with the hope only a desperate mother could muster. I was going to be escorted to the Waldorf-Astoria Hotel confectionary, a highfalutin place where the rich rub shoulders with the rich, and where someone like me would need to hitch a ride on the coattails of someone like Charlie Harrison to be allowed inside. So to her this was going to be money well spent. The shoes hurt the minute I put them on. They were tight in the toe box, and too short for my still-growing feet. But these were the ones she wanted for me, so I slipped on the party shoes, and with that tossed aside every ounce of good sense my mother ever wished she had given me. She had plans. We both had plans. In New York City.

New York City has run its course. Every bit of it will one day decay back into the rotten ground from whence it came two-bit brick by two-bit brick. I wish I'd known yesterday what I knew today. That all good girls, who once hoped and dreamt big, knew that a thing hoped for diminishes before your very eyes the moment it is wished for, and that anything worth having should be appreciated for what it is. Sixteen years didn't teach me the ways of the world. I knew better than to pin my hopes on days that might not come, and this is why I felt my birthday night was mine to do with as I wished. It was mine, after all. Wasn't it? Moments seized become experiences that no one can take from you, and overlooked shoes sitting in a dusty torn box on a dime-store shelf only become undervalued if forgotten. If Ma thought this she didn't say.

I hated those new shoes. I wouldn't tell Ma this. I would tell her that I really was the envy, because I was. That the shoes helped me dance the best, because they did. That the wine stains would come out easily. That this was arguably the happiest sixteenth birthday party a girl has ever had. I would share only the details of the night that she would understand: that orchids die, that soda drinks get spiked, and that curls fall. I wouldn't tell her that Charlie couldn't be responsible for me. She would never have agreed, but that down-on-his-luck Charlie wasn't capable of accompanying a sixteen-year-old girl, on the verge of becoming a woman, to a hotel candy counter. He was just a boy.

I turned images from the night before over in my mind like the clattering wheel, the worn handle, and the memory began to sharpen as the champagne fog lifted. There was a pair of unwanted shoes, a missing pair of perspiration-stained white gloves, and a torn frock. I lay down uneasily on an aging settee in a hotel foyer too tangled to move. There was a dark-haired man, not Charlie, lying in a tousled bed upstairs too drunk to know who spent the night with him, but I knew. The wheel continued to grind. My mind returned to the dark-paneled room and to the sun-kissed man.

Sunlight awakened sooty glass panes as it streamed through the oversized arched windows into the hotel foyer and made elongated geometric patterns on the black-and-white tiled floor. I tucked my swollen feet under me, curled up into a ball, and closed my eyes so that I could see more clearly. A mother should be out looking for her daughter when she realizes she has not come home, but only if she is your ma. My ma would not be out searching near empty streets, under-lit alleyways, nor rain-swollen gutters. She would not frantically inquire about me by telephone, or telegram, or by some desperate knock on a stranger's door simply because she trusted Charlie, Charlie's pedigree, and Charlie's overpriced orchid corsage.

If I tell you how Charlie Harrison, of all people, wound up bringing me to my destiny on the night of my sixteenth birthday, June 17, 1922, will you promise me you will take off your ill-fitting shoes and pull up a chair? I have one for the story books. Charlies are a dime a dozen and men like the one in the corner suite deserve recognition and to have their stories told. Not because they seduce, and can make a young girl's life a living hell if she winds up pregnant and thrown out onto the street, but because dapper men in the very prime of their life, like the expensive-looking man from the upstairs apartment, see only nothing in a world too blinded by nothings, and are wanting something. Like me.

II

Ma eyed the party shoes, I thought, running my slender fingers over the wine stains, like the eye of a hungry hawk on an unsuspecting chick. She found them sitting in a broken box on the top shelf of a Woolworth's lost in semi-darkness. In shadow. When she spied that dusty brown box she cried, "Edie!" and pulled in her breath sharply. "Would you just look!"

"At what, Ma?" I answered, dusting off the boxes at eye level.

"Just looky there. Right there. Right in 'em shadows. Baby, look," she cried again. "Get up there and get me that box."

"That old one?"

"Get up there."

"Shouldn't we ask..."

"And let 'em know they've got somethin' in here they shouldn't be havin'? Absolutely not. Besides. We're dealin' with the hoi polloi down here. Says so right up there on that sign."

I turned to look at the mottled cardboard sign which read SELF-SERVICE in faded red letters. "I don't understand, Ma."

"That's no ordinary box," she chirped. "You see any other box in this piss-poor store lookin' anythin' like that one up there?"

8

I looked at the display of drab-colored boxes and answered her. "I don't see anything else looking like it. Not in here."

"That's because this," she said, pointing to what we could now see was a bright orange box the closer we inspected it and our eyes began adjusting to the dim light, "ain't some five-and-dime box." Curious, I pulled on the wooden stepladder and positioned it closer to the box. "If my suspicions is correct we got us a find," Ma squealed. "And it might be gold! Got that? No one deserves this more than you, baby girl. And on your birthday!" She said this with the sing-song voice of a child herself.

I did as Ma said and stepped up onto that paint-splattered ladder, but only because I really was curious. The air was thick with dust and I pushed it away with a wave of my hand. The box was broken. It fell apart in my hands when I took ahold of it, but it was once a beautiful sculpted box with capitalized chocolate brown letters displayed across the top. I ran my fingers over the expensive department store words. "It says Bonwit Teller."

"Open it," she begged.

I lifted the lid and let it fall to the floor. Ma threw her hands to her underfed hips and stood on the tips of her toes to peer inside. "Mother Mary," she sang. "I knew it." I looked at her crossly. Mother Mary wasn't having anything to do with this and I didn't think Ma should be using her name that way. "Get down from there before you fall," she croaked. "Try 'em on. Try 'em," she chimed, pulling out a flimsy grey shoebox from the shelf. She emptied it and shoved a pair of ugly black pumps and the broken Bonwit Teller box back onto the shelf where they disappeared into the dark.

The shoes were stiff, brand new, and had never been worn. I touched the satin lining with my slender fingers and paused. These shoes were going to be too good for me. Too posh. I could never wear them. Ma put her hands on her hips once more and then snuck a quick look behind her. "Try 'em, Edie," she urged.

"I don't know, Ma. I'm not..."

Ma took one of the shoes, knelt down before me, and like a knight playing his dutiful part in the quest, pushed that errant shoe onto my foot. "We're buyin' these," she pronounced, quite satisfied with herself. I kicked off the shoe and frowned, but Ma stuffed those slippers down into the borrowed box and closed the lid with a definitive slap.

I complained. "They're too small."

"You buttered piece of French toast. All fat and full of air. These," she said purring, "are your ticket outta here."

<>

We stepped away from the peeling red linoleum floor, from the rancid smell of body odor, and out into the afternoon light. It hit me squarely in the eye and I lifted a hand to my face. "I know you think I'm a thief," said Ma, taking my arm and pulling me down the pinched sidewalk. "But no one's a thief when they're payin' their dime for what *obviously* no one else wants. You got that?"

"I don't want them," I tried.

Surprised, Ma looked up at me and complained. "Don't want 'em? Of course you want 'em. Charlie's takin' you high-steppin', baby girl. Got that? And high-steppin' requires high-steppin'."

She demonstrated by picking up her battered brown boats and stepping over the cracks in the sidewalk. "Don't doubt your ma now. I know a thing or two about 'em fancy shops. The ones we can't never afford."

"That's a double negative, Ma."

"Oh hush your mouth. No one asked you about my words, wise head. Them's mine." She hugged the shoes tighter to her chest.

"You practice using my words," I offered, "and see if you don't get yourself a seat at the Waldorf-Astoria candy counter." I rolled my eyes. "With Charlie Harrison."

"I'm offended," she barked. "I made this happen, you know." She put her hand to her heart and said some kind of prayer as she looked up at Woolworth's fraying red awning.

"It's going to be too posh, Ma," I complained. "Are you certain this is a good idea?"

Ma raised her voice. "Goin' to be posh? Of course it's goin' to be posh. Isn't that the whole idea? Isn't it time you went someplace, baby girl?" she chided, pulling me away from the leering shadow of the bulging brick building.

"But I am someplace, Ma," I said, sweeping my hand down the street indicating the familiar tenement buildings with their broken facades, peeling window sills, and overpopulated stoops. "Where else would I go?" We passed a tobacco shop and I peered inside. There were three young men dressed down in soiled t-shirts smoking Luckies, smacking cards, and sharing some joke. They laughed and hit their hardscrabble hands to their knees. I was still looking over the men as we continued walking past, and their eyes, now turned eagle, were looking onto me.

Ma snorted and pulled me away. "You never gonna see your-self steppin' out on a Broadway stage, Edie? Hoofin' it with all the other pretties? Makin' yourself useful?"

"No, Ma," I complained. Stepping onto the balls of my feet, I skipped across the busy cobblestone street, nearly getting hit by one of the lumbering delivery vans. I turned around and shook my head at the driver, but he threw out a greasy hand to dismiss me. I wasn't going to have this conversation again. Ma ran up beside me, shoved her thin arm into the crook of mine, and purred. "No, Ma," I continued. "No. Why would I want that?" I argued. "Broadway's too big. Too grand. Too...something, Ma. I don't even know."

Ma softened. "It's not for you to say, baby. It's on Mrs. Harrison now." She looked at me and winked.

I turned away from her and lifted my feet over a discarded wad of wet newspaper. I had no use for the news, unlike Mr. Jaffee, the fish seller, who used the papers to wrap up the day's catch. His papers were always littering the sidewalk forcing us to sidestep rotting remnants of mackerel or cod. "I said I'm going, Ma." I rolled my eyes again and made a sour face. "But Charlie?" Ma barked out more tunes about opportunity, heritage, and horse racing. "I said I'd go." I looked down on her definitively. "But only this one time."

Ma shuffled her short legs next to mine as we passed the greengrocer. There were two dark-haired men, the Moroz brothers, standing side-by-side in the doorway dressed in their matching white aprons shooing away some child's dirty hand from their wares. They moved in unison over their worn wooden tables as if their lumbering bodies were doing a deep knee-bending Cossack's dance. I wanted to pluck one of their fat cabbages right out from under their watchful eyes and give it to the child. He was hungry. As we passed by they looked me up and down and then folded their pimply arms across their bulging bellies. Ma and I shared a look for we both knew there was no getting fat on boiled cabbage.

I turned around to look at the Russian dancers one more time even though what I was looking for wasn't here. I knew that. Ma took my arm again, sternly, as we continued tripping over one another's sentences. Me complaining about Charlie's pimples and his two left feet, and Ma promising me that Mr. Florenz Ziegfeld was personally scouring the streets looking for pretties. I would never believe her when she told me, repeatedly, that I was good enough for the stage. Because I wasn't. When I finally let myself find the right words, the words I knew Ma was waiting to hear, I spun them out as best I could like candied sugar on a stick. "Thank you," I lied, "for the party shoes, Ma. They're just what I wanted. Everyone coming to the candy counter will love them."

Ma smiled buoyantly and pointed her toes as if she was the one stepping out onto a Broadway stage making a spectacle of herself. "They're better than anythin' anyone else will have. Got that? And I acquired them," she said, pausing to admire the shoes. She was proud of herself, and her choice of words, I could tell. "Just like your pa always said, Edie. 'What goes 'round comes 'round.'" She was remembering Pa. "And to think we got ourselves a piece of yesterday's finery." She pronounced it *fine-er-ee*. Like *yes-sir-ee*. "Still lookin' top notch."

I couldn't help but remember him too. I was always remembering Pa. I pulled her in close and gave her a a playful tug on her arm. My ma. If only Mr. Ziegfeld would find her he'd see how irresistible she could be with those sparkling blue eyes. Despite the long hot days she spends on her hands and knees, those eyes still shine brighter than any one of Mr. Ziegfeld's stars. We both turned this time and craned our necks to look at one of the blackened fire escapes that came down the side of a listing tar-covered building. We scanned it, without missing a step, taking our eyes all the way up to the greying laundry on the roof and then dropping them back down again. As I pushed for a closer look, Ma pulled.

New York City, without a doubt, is what you find it to be. If you find it to be good, then New York City will be good. If you find it to be your due, well, then New York City becomes your due, but personally, I find the city sleepy. They say it is the city that never sleeps, what with all the dancing, follies, back alley parties, bootleg whiskey, and girls. Sleepy, I imagine, not because everyone is sleeping off some rabble-rousing gin-soaked night, but because no one has a mind of their own.

"You know, Ma," I tried, "if it wasn't for you cleaning those dance floors and polishing them up the way Mrs. Harrison likes, I never would have needed a new pair of party shoes."

Ma stopped in her tracks and looked me in the eye. "You go to this birthday party, Edie, and you take my advice. I seen the way Mrs. Harrison looks at you. She wants somethin' from you."

"I don't like the way Charlie looks at me."

"Oh pshaw," she hooted. "Charlie's the one to get you outta this hellhole."

"He's fourteen, Ma. His voice hasn't even changed."

"That's enough, Edie. He's gonna make you shine. Now listen."

I looked beyond the narrow row of raked buildings and squinted into the bright blue sky. "You're dreaming, Ma."

"Mrs. Harrison has 'em emerald eyes on you," she continued. "For whatever reason she got, and that woman, she got a reason." She winked again. "Might be she wants you for her boy."

I shook my head. "She's only using me," I explained, extending my sinewy thin arms to Ma and showing her the waltz step, "for display." I was beginning to realize just what kind of place Harrison's Dance Emporium was turning out to be. Sure, it was a place for high-steppin' it with the well-heeled, but at what cost? There I could do what I did best, which was to dance, but only so that Mrs. Harrison could do what she did best, which was to show off. Ma was just as eager to make sure Mrs. Harrison still had what it took to look the part, and somehow they both thought this was going to be on me. I looked at the way Ma was holding onto those brand new shoes. It was as if she was clutching gold.

Ma turned to look at me. If she knew what I was thinking she didn't say. She was unapologetic and she spit out the words as though for all my life she'd been waiting for this moment to say them. "You know I can't afford you." It sounded like she was spitting out the taste of rotten egg on toast. I was stunned, my eyes wide, but her words were clear.

"Ma!" I cried. "What are you saying?"

This time she paused. I watched her scan the street as if she was still looking for Pa when she turned back abruptly and pounced, "You're costing me too much, Edie."

"But Ma, I'm doing what I do best. What I want to do..."

"You you you," she complained, pulling on my arm sharply.

We stepped wide behind a dawdling old brown mare. "Ma! Not Charlie. Not anyone. Not now, Ma. Please. Not while I'm still waiting..."

Ma winced. "I've been at 'em floors for sixteen years, Edie. Sixteen. Puttin' you right. Givin' you everythin' a ma can give her baby girl. Youdogoodbymeyouhear," she said, talking so fast and sharp her jumbled words spilled out like rosary beads knotted on a string. "You do good. You do right. Youdorightforme."

We were both jarred suddenly when we came upon a dark-haired man, probably about Pa's age, stretched out on one of the broken crates along the sidewalk. He was dressed in a pair of soiled coveralls reading a crisp white newspaper, not just studying the thin pages feigning interest, but reading them with concerted effort. He wasn't turning the newspaper over in disgust like Pa used to do. I couldn't help but notice how he lifted his coal-colored eyes to me when we passed. I shuddered. This was as close as we'd ever come to seeing someone who looked like Pa.

"I will do good, Ma," I promised, stumbling. "I know what you've sacrificed, but not marriage. Please. It's not for me." Ma shooed me away with a calloused hand as she turned to take another quick peek at the man. He lifted a lock of his hair with a dirt-stained fingernail and nodded. "I know it hasn't been easy going without, and all for me, but I promise you I'll take on more responsibility." How many times had I said these very words? Too many.

Ma turned us away from the man. She lifted her hand and ran it down the length of my dark ringlet curls. "Then you take 'em dance steps someplace," she said. It wasn't a suggestion. "Or you do right and marry." But I cringed. I wanted her to stop pushing me up onto some Broadway marquee or pushing me right back into Charlie's jodhpurs. Didn't she know that what I wanted was right here? "I don't know just what sights Mrs. Harrison's got for you with her Charlie," she continued, "but 'em sights is what God's gonna be doin' right. And it might be she's groomin' you, like one of her overpriced fillies, for her boy." Ma snorted. "I'm gonna be needin' God too, Edie. For once."

I know my ma, and she would have dropped to her knees right there on the sidewalk if she dared. "God. You gonna be doin' us right," she barked. Ma clawed around into the pocket of her smock for her rosary and lifted it to the sky. "Got that. 'Em's mighty words." She was missing one of her bottom teeth. "Yessir," she sang, pulling me in close. "You gonna outshine all 'em fancy girls. All of 'em. You hear me? We got luck. All 'em dancin' lessons. 'Em party lessons. All 'em books." She looked at me, and in all seriousness said, "Be gettin' on now with your life, Edie, the way God intended. It's time."

"No Ma," I winced. "You're telling me to go? Why? I won't. I can't."

She turned around again and gave that man the longest look I'd ever seen her give any one of the men we'd passed. Disappointment after disappointment, day after day, but this one could have been my pa. It just could have been. "You did somethin' right to please that old bat," she continued. "I don't know what she sees, but she sees it. Got that? You got yourself your own star, Edie, but Mrs. Harrison...I know her. She's gonna see to it that star shines brightest." Ma put her arm around my narrow waist and I saw that she had acquired another tear in her smock, the baby blue one covered in faded red and white chrysanthemums. "Foryouyessir," she sang, slipping her words together again. "That's God's work, baby girl. And God is right where you are."

<>

God was not here, I winced, looking into the panes of early morning light dancing on the black-and-white mosaic tiled floor of the Waldorf-Astoria Hotel. He left me sometime around midnight.

III

I heard the treacle in his voice before I saw him. "Miss?" he offered. I sat up expectantly. Had Pa returned? The boy's face was so close to mine I could smell the staleness of his breath.

"Jesus," I shouted, startled. Awakened.

"Do you need my help?" he asked, reaching for my hand with his white-gloved one. "I'm here to help." He spoke rapidly, just like Ma, in that haunted Italian version of some great-grandmother's past.

"Who are you?" I complained, stirring and lifting my eyes to the sound of his anxious voice. I was looking into the cobalt blue eyes of a stranger who, in turn, was looking down on me. This boy was not my pa, but I listened to the familiar sweet drippings his words made. I ran the images through my mind. Taffy. Vice. Wheel. Gin. Sometime in that moment between looking at the sunlight as it made irregular shapes through a set of yellowing lace curtains on the floor, and his incessant tapping on my shoulder, I must have fallen asleep. "Who are you?" I asked again. He seemed mesmerized by the way my ankle-length frock had lifted beyond my shins and was now riding up over my knees. I pulled it down as his eyes went up and down my slender body.

He extended a hand to my elbow in an attempt to right me. "You can't sleep here. What with the manager. And all the eyes on you. What room is it, Miss? I'll help you."

My mind was reaching for an answer, but there was last night's champagne, the gentleman's locked door, and the dancing shoes. I looked down to make sure the shoes were still where I left them. They were on the floor, covered in dark wine stains, and tipped on their sides, deflated. His bright eyes followed mine to the shoes.

"I saw you last night," he whispered. "I saw it all."

I shot him a look of surprise. His fraying blue cap was lopsided, probably thrown over his dark curls in haste, and he looked at me this time as though there was some secret between us. "You?"

He took my hand, squeezed it playfully, and pulled me up from the uncomfortable citrine settee. "No. Mr. Andino," he whispered.

"You?" I asked. "You're too young to be a mister." My stocking feet slipped on the slick tile and the boy threw an arm around my waist to keep me from falling.

"I saw you last night. With him," he said. "We all did. High-steppin' it. But you need to go back to your room, Miss." He spoke with a new sense of urgency. I racked my brain for the word I would use if I were to describe his voice. I settled on staccato.

"I haven't...," I started to say.

His blue gems danced when he talked. I watched his eyes dart about the empty hotel foyer before settling back down on me. "I'll bring you the Bromo? An aspirin?"

I struggled to stand. "No," I said uncertain. "No, thank you. I'll go."

"You got the whole world on your shoulders," he offered. His eyes darted about the vaulted room before he turned them back to me. He looked into me, undressing me in his mind, I thought, as he put those eyes on my breasts, my thighs, my feet.

"I haven't," I said uneasily. I extended a hand to steady myself on one of the marbled columns filling out the room. "I haven't anything at all."

"Girls," he offered smiling. "So young."

"I'm sixteen," I said offended.

The boy looked down on me and chuckled. "So easy being a girl." I shot him a look of distrust, but he laughed. One of his dark curls came loose from under the cap as he leaned down to pick up my shoes. "You're even better lookin' up close and in person," he said, securing his arm around my waist and escorting me across the floor. I took a giant step from one of the patterned carpets, tossed decoratively over the tiles, to another. The worn carpets littered the floor like paper trash littering Fifth Avenue. "I have a sister, and golly, what she'd give for these shoes. To be in your shoes."

I looked down at my stocking feet. "Why does everyone keep saying that?" I asked, taking the shoes from him.

The boy blushed. "Miss Agnes Ayres, you sure do it smart. Just like her. We all thought you were her. Or maybe you are, you know, her, but you...you're just, oh, I don't know."

He looked at me as if he was inspecting a piece of the high-class hotel statuary. "Same dark curls, same eyes, same chin." He laughed and I could see the way this pleased him.

I frowned. "What are you talking about?"

"But you might need more luck, Miss." The wheels in his mind turned and he looked at me as though continuing to undress me with his overeager eyes.

"Luck?"

The boy smiled. "Maybe you should go back to your room before the detectives chase you out." I shot him a look of genuine surprise. "You're not in any kind of jam," he explained. "Nothin' like that. No. Not you. It's just that...well...you never know who'll be gettin' the boot these days. And I can't let it be you." I looked at him and smiled warily. "Used to be women couldn't be down here alone. It didn't bode well, you know. Or look good in the eyes of others." He was struggling to tell me I might be mistaken for a prostitute. "But times are changin', you know."

"No, I don't know."

The boy's blush was brighter. "You're in one of the finer hotels, Miss, but you know that. And we have rules. What with sleepin' outside the room and all. Don't mind me," he whispered. "I don't mind what you do. Or don't do." I frowned. "Come on," he said, taking my elbow in his hand and steering me away from a hodgepodge of mismatched parlor chairs. "What room?"

I pulled away from him. "I haven't a room."

"Oh," he said, averting his eyes. "No room?"

"No. Where's Charlie?"

"Who?"

I ran my hands down my lemon-colored party frock to smooth it out. "Charlie Harrison."

"Oh...Mr. Harrison," he said whistling. "That high hat."

"He's not a mister. He's Charlie," I complained. "His mother bought me this dress from Macy's. She made me come here last night to the confectionary. It was, maybe, a date," I explained. "Something like that." He nodded. "It was supposed to be for my birthday." There were dark shadows falling to the floor and the boy steered me away. I reached out my hands to steady myself as we sidestepped them. "She said I was ready for this," I winced, with a wave of my hand over the imposing hotel foyer, "but I don't know. I think I was improperly escorted."

The boy squinted and looked down at the ruffled neckline of the tea-length frock. I wasn't sure if it was a question or an approval. He continued to touch my elbow, far too intimately, and put his lips to my ear. "But it was you who skipped out on Mr. Harrison in the confectionary. Or was it in the ballroom?" he asked.

I pulled away. "I know what I did."

He stood up straighter, and with a false sense of formality said, "Mr. Harrison's car came for him sometime around eleven. Last evenin'."

I looked at him incredulously. "Then where were you? Why didn't you tell him to wait?"

"Mr. Harrison, Miss? Wait for you?"

"Oh never mind," I complained, raking my hands through my disheveled curls. "I need a cab."

The boy leaned into me. "Mr. Andino will get you a car."

His breath was probably sour from last night's beer. I took a step away from him. Things were all still so muddled. "Who?"

He raised an eyebrow. "I'll see to it that things are discreet, Miss. For you."

I spun around and looked once more at the spacious Waldorf-Astoria Hotel foyer, filled to the brim with worn velvet furniture positioned against the paneled walls of imposing marble. There was an overattentive use of tables and chairs needlessly arranged as if the Waldorf-Astoria was expecting a hundred people to be sitting in the room at one time. "Take me to him," I said anxiously. He led me past one of the towering potted palms jutting out of a decorative Ming urn and I swatted it with the back of my hand.

"Oh, I can't do that, Miss."

"Why not?"

"Mr. Andino is gone."

I placed both feet on the floor to try and regain my balance. "Gone? What do you mean?"

"London, I think, Miss. He was picked up about...um...an hour ago."

"Why didn't you stop him?"

"Me?"

"You've got your hand clawing mine," I complained, pulling away abruptly. "Why didn't you tell me? I have a grievance with him. With this hotel."

The boy appeared baffled. "Tell you what, Miss?"

"Oh my god, you are worse than French toast," I complained. "I don't know why you didn't tell me."

"I'm tellin' you now, Miss. Mr. Andino was here, but now he's gone. To the docks."

"When will he be back?"

Without emotion he answered, "That I wouldn't know."

"I don't believe you."

He looked down my frock as if peering inside for the department store label and frowned. His eyes settled on a tear along the neckline. "No room. No service," he recited, "but here I am willin' to help you. Even offerin' to get you a car."

"Stop it," I complained, sitting down in one of the sagging chairs. There were numerous small tears all along the velvet-covered arms and I picked at several of the threads. "Leave me alone. I need to think."

"But..."

"I said leave me alone. Please," I added. "I've been wronged."

"It's almost nine, Miss. People will be gettin' up soon and you can't..."

"I can do whatever I choose to do. This isn't your hotel."

"No, Miss, but I am employed..."

"Please leave," I said, looking at him crossly. "I mean it. I can be here. There's no law against it." I was coming undone at the thought that I had just spent the night with a gentleman who was too drunk to ask me my name, but not so drunk that he would miss his ocean voyage the following morning. "What time is it?"

"I just told you. Almost nine, Miss."

"What time did Mr. ...Mr. Andino," I croaked, mispronouncing his name, "depart?"

"Eight, Miss."

"And what time did I...," I wondered.

The boy smiled. "You were in his room until half past six."

I hissed, "Go away."

He took my hand in his again and whispered, "I'm helpin' you."

"Then get me to the pier," I said, correcting him. "Docks are for laborers."

The boy grinned, showing a gap between his two front teeth. "You won't catch him. The ship sails at nine," he chirped, looking at the imposing gilded hotel clock standing, sentry-like, in the foyer.

I stood and looked up at him. "Liar!" I shouted. I tried stuffing my feet back into the party shoes but my toes were too swollen to fit. "I hate these shoes," I cursed, tossing them onto one of the paltry chairs.

"Come on," he said, grabbing the shoes and urging me toward the door. "You need to go before the rest of the hotel wakes up." I stood on the tips of my toes thinking it might help me look taller and therefore in charge of myself, but he still towered over me. So I turned it around on him and looked down at his scuffed boots.

"What pay class are you?" I asked. He looked taken aback. "You're not a bellboy, are you? You're something else," I reasoned, scrutinizing his over-starched navy blue suit. It was well-worn and had acquired an undesirable sheen. "You work for Mr. Andino, don't you?" He hesitated and pulled on the sleeves of his box-shaped jacket. I noticed that one of the brass buttons was missing. "You work for him and you're supposedly doing me a favor, aren't you? Escorting me out of the hotel and getting me into a car? But that's on him, isn't it?" The boy didn't answer. "Isn't it?" I demanded.

The jacket was too small and he pulled on the sleeves once more. "I work for Mr. Andino, and for the entire floor, but..."

"I knew it!"

I took the shoes, now darkened with perspiration, from him and pushed my way over the abundant patterned carpets. The tiled floor was decorated with small black medallions, and I leapt from one to the other as I danced past the reception desk and into the narrow elevator. "Mr. Andino's room," I barked. The elevator attendant nodded sleepily and pulled the black metal gate closed with a white-gloved hand.

"You can't disturb him," the boy insisted, opening the gate and stepping inside. "Mr. Andino is a very important man. Top brass. The cat's meow."

I cringed. "So important that he would get me a car?"

"Take care of you," the boy corrected.

"Take care of me, my ass," I hissed. "And to think I was going to let him get away with it."

The boy shuddered. "Yeah, but that's because you know the game, Miss."

"For the love of god," I squealed. "Are you out of your mind? This isn't a game." The elevator attendant looked as though she was waiting for the boy to step away, and when he didn't she closed the metal gate, pulled the wooden door closed, and ran her hand over the brass lever. The elevator crept heavenward toward the second floor. With a trembling hand I touched the walls when it came to an abrupt stop. The attendant opened the steel cage and I looked back at her as I stumbled out of the coffin-like box. I wasn't wearing my shoes, but this didn't seem to faze her. She smoothed out her long brown skirt and blushed.

The boy looked as if he was going to be sick. "You should have taken the stairs."

I held the shoes by their untied bows and tossed them over my shoulder like a peddler carrying a sack of worn goods. "My feet hurt. Besides, only the help take the stairs," I winced. "Got that? You had no business being in that elevator with me. It isn't respectable. She should have known better."

"Maybe she thought you were invitin' me in. Because I'm helpin'."

"What could I possibly want from you?"

<>

Each of the dark-paneled doors on the second floor looked alike, but I searched the hallway and found a calling card with his name, MR. LAWRENCE ANDINO, printed on it in bold black type. Someone had slipped the card into a little brass bracket on the front of the apartment door. I rapped urgently and the sound reverberated angrily down the empty hall. The boy complained. "You can't wake him," he yelped, pulling me away from the door. "Don't you know the rules, Miss? Don't get me sacked. Please."

I tried the gold-embossed knob, but the door was locked. "I was going to go home, you know. Just leave. As if no part of me belonged upstairs in this kind of apartment. But not now," I winced, rapping urgently on the door. "There are too many girls coming down here getting lost. Got that? We're getting lost at the party."

The boy pulled me away from the door. "Stop! You don't want the hotel detectives on you, do you, Miss?"

"There I was minding my own business," I trilled, "sleeping off a thimble of champagne, and you push this...this cockamamy story on me that Mr. Andino is doing me a favor by getting me a car. You're crass," I said, turning to him. "I bet you don't even know what that word means."

"Stop knockin'," he urged, pulling on my arm. "I mean it." He shot a worried look down the hall. "We have standards. Do you want to get caught?"

I howled. "Standards? Bringing unsuspecting girls up to this hotel floor, the poshest of them all, I bet. Am I right? Bringing up all those bottles of smuggled French wine for Mr. Andino. Jesus, Mary, and Joseph," I said, cursing my mother under my breath. I turned to the boy and hissed. "This is all your fault. Double-crossing me."

He grabbed my hand. "I said stop it. You'll wake the dead."

"No, I won't. They'll sleep through anything in their gilded cages," I answered sardonically. "What with their eiderdown, their tapestries, and drawn curtains." I laughed cruelly. "I've seen what that cage looks like." I was beginning to recall images from Mr. Andino's room. There was a black marble fireplace, a bit of polished jousting armor standing upright next to it, and a sharp lance tucked neatly away into a corner. I wasn't sure what it was I wanted from him or why I was still here, knocking terribly, but I had been wronged. That much I knew.

"I don't know what you're talking about, Miss. We're the finest..."

I swallowed hard. The bitterness of this pill was almost too much. "You want to know something? I've never slept on a canopied bed as big as the one in there. Never. My ma, my mother," I said, correcting myself, "and I share one room. I sleep in a crib. Got that? A crib. Pa left us three years ago to go find some relative of his with an inheritance, but he's probably been scalped somewhere out in Nebraska. My ma deserves this," I said, running my hand down the dark grooved wooden doorframe. "She deserves this."

The boy held my trembling hand in his. "I'm sorry," he said. "Truly. I'll get you a room if you'll just stop yelpin'. Come on," he barked, pulling me down the hall. "I have the key."

IV

My heart raced with the turn of the brass key in the door. My very own room, I thought, taking a running leap across the flowered carpets and onto the double bed. The overused iron bed sagged in the middle, but I fell into the depression and lay on the white quilt quite satisfied. The room was painted the same dreary salmon color as Mr. Andino's room, but there was something obviously more feminine about this one. The patterned carpets, scattered about the room, were light in color. There were classical urns and a smattering of potted palms positioned along one of the long walls. Once again, there seemed to be an overabundant use of tables. Each one stood alone in the room and was draped with a fringed silk cloth.

I looked up at the imposing carved wardrobe listing ever so slightly to one side. It was scratched somewhat on the painted tangerine-colored doors and clashed terribly with the rest of the dismal room. It was as if someone had been searching for a new look by painting the dark cupboard, but obviously they had missed their mark. There were remnants of a floral wallpaper panel on one of the walls next to the fireplace and I couldn't help but notice how faded it had become. Although I would have hoped for a suite as large as the one I stayed in last night, outfitted with a cozy dark-paneled room filled from floor to ceiling with clothbound books and a pair of crossed cavalry sabers, I turned over on the bed and looked at the boy.

"This will do," I said flatly.

He bowed. "It's Tom, Miss."

"You serve this floor?" He bowed again. "And you help damsels in distress?"

"No, Miss. Just you."

"Me?"

"Yes, Miss. You have a need."

"A need?" I looked at him and laughed. "I guess I do, don't I?" I slipped under the starched sheets and pulled the quilt up to my chin. I heard Tom gasp, but he said nothing. "You'll come for me, Tom, when Mr. Andino wakes up." It wasn't a question. "I have a grievance." He kept his eyes on me and on the bed. "I said: You'll come for me."

Tom stood before me, awkwardly. He shuffled his boots on the old wooden floor sweeping away some imaginary scratch. "Mr. Andino is a very wealthy man, Miss," he croaked. "I'll try."

"He's a coward. Do you know that?" I explained. "I never should have let him take over."

"No, Miss."

"He's a coward for using me." I burped and covered my mouth with the back my sweating palm. I was beginning to feel like I might throw up last night's wine. "All of you," I complained. Tom put his wide eyes on the floor. He paused for so long I thought he was counting the threads in the carpet. "Stop bowing. Please," I added reluctantly.

"I'm not obliged to serve you, Miss, but I am tryin' to help."

"Whose apartment is this?" I asked, slipping off the bed and stepping into the white-tiled bathroom, one of the true wonders of the Waldorf-Astoria. The tiles were showing their age with hairline cracks, but so what. "Imagine it. My own bathroom," I squealed.

"Don't touch anything, Miss," warned Tom, taking an uncertain step toward the private bathroom. "The Madame will return tomorrow."

"Oh, the Madame," I sang, staring at my bloodshot eyes in the large gilded mirror and chiding him. "But for now, Tom, it's mine. Isn't it?" I looked at my reflection and pulled up the images from the night before. The sodas. The parade. The barrage of flashing cameras. I turned away from the memory of it all and tiptoed across the room. I ran my hand over each of the tables and fingered the aubergine cloths just as if I were stepping across my own apartment floor and running my hand over the well-worn wooden table, the abundant flies, and the tin plates.

Tom coughed. "One hour, Miss. That's all. One hour and I'll see what I can do to get you an appointment with Mr. Andino."

I shot him a look of disgust. "An appointment? My god, Tom. I spent the night with the man." I moved away from him and looked out the second-story window and onto the empty Sunday morning street below. "Do you know I never cursed until last night." I ran my manicured hands down my thin face. "I have on nail lacquer," I said. "Imagine. Charlie told me it was sinful, but Ma insisted I paint my short nails red." I saw Tom shake his head. "You know she washes floors in one of those society dance halls for the hobnobbing set, but we live on the lower end," I explained. "Imagine. Ma and I come all the way up here in the wee hours of the morning, in the dark, so I can have party lessons." Tom nodded again, uneasily. He turned to look at the shoes which were lying in a forgotten heap on the floor. "My Ma. A washerwoman. I bet she's never seen a bathroom like that. Not that big. Not that clean."

"So you really don't belong in the motion pictures?" asked Tom. "I mean we all thought..."

"I don't know where I belong," I realized. "We can barely afford the tram up here, but sometimes one has to go without sardines," I continued, sweeping my hands down the sides of the yellow chiffon searching for the buttons. I fingered another tear, pulled on the memory of just when and how the frock got torn, and unbuttoned it. I returned to the bathroom. "Imagine. My very own clawfoot tub."

"Don't," he balked, taking a step toward me.

"Don't use these?" I trilled, marveling at the handsome set of clean white towels. "Of course I'm going to use these. I'm going to take a hot soak," I explained. I waved Tom away with a flick of my hand. "My rules now. Now that you're in my bathroom."

"This isn't yours, Miss. I only thought if I could help..."

I lifted my wide eyes to him and smiled. "I was only just burrowed down in that uncomfortable old sofa working up the courage to ask someone, anyone, for fifty cents for taxi fare when low and behold a liberated senator... you," I chimed, "rescues me and brings me up to my very own private room. I don't want anything," I tried. "Not a thing." The words spilled out from somewhere, some overheard script, and Tom stood up straighter.

He bowed. "Ice, Miss?"

I shook my head. "No. Come for me the moment Mr. Andino stirs." I raced back to the bed and leapt onto it.

"I'll leave you then, Miss," said Tom, setting his jaw straight.

"It's Edie. Edie May," I chirped, peeking out from behind the quilt.

Tom looked down on me but didn't say a word. No "Pleased to meet you, Miss May," or "Glad to be of your service, Miss May." Nothing. Finally, I coaxed a word from him by hopping off the bed and drawing the ivory lace curtains closed. "Don't mess up anything," he croaked. "Promise. I can't get sacked."

"Roger," I said saluting.

"It's Tom," he complained, backing out of the room.

"You really are French toast," I trilled, hopping on the bed and covering myself up with the quilt.

"If you want to look at the paper, Miss, I can bring it to you while you wait," he offered, taking a step backwards, but obviously dawdling. He cleared his throat. "That was some weddin' banquet last night. We all thought so. Somethin' special seeing you there. Here. In all your finery," he added, indicating the shoes.

I turned my nose up at the idea of the paper. "You were there? You saw me?"

Tom nodded. "I told you I saw it all last night. First the chocolate malts. Then the sodas. All that dancin'."

I peeked out from under the quilt and frowned. "You never told me."

"You were certainly the belle of the..."

I sat up. "I wasn't with Charlie then, was I?"

"For part of the evening, Miss, but then..."

"Milk toast," I complained. "And stuffed like a Christmas sausage. Do you know how many chocolate malts that insipid boy drank?" I answered for him. "Three."

Tom nodded uneasily. "But when he followed you he found you dancin' at the weddin' banquet. In the ballroom. When we all thought..." He paused and looked down on me, curiously. "Just about every gentleman in that room got the chance to take a turn with you, didn't they?"

I cringed. "Charlie ruined my steps cutting in like that. You're not supposed to do that. Not over and over. It's wrong," I explained. "It's called monopolizing. You'd think his mother would have taught him a thing or two about partner dancing before strapping me onto him for the evening." Tom opened the door and looked uneasily down the hall. I leaned in and continued. "I always thought when you tied the knot, and you said a word or two of 'I do,' that was it. You might take a photograph or curl your hair for the occasion, but my stars, what a charade." I burped. "I never thought I'd lose Charlie, though, through it all."

Tom clicked his heels and turned again, anxiously, to look down the hall. "Better weddin' charades have never before been had. Not when someone like you partakes." If he was overcome by it all I couldn't tell.

I shot him a worried look. "I didn't do anything wrong, you know. It was dreary sitting in the confectionary." Tom clicked his heels again and took a step backwards. I looked at him with doe-like eyes. "I don't know what came over me. I just wanted to see what all the fuss was about in the ballroom. That's all."

"Don't switch on the electric light," Tom cautioned me, "or let anyone know you're here. I can't get the boot."

I frowned. "I didn't do anything wrong. Even you said so. Even the bride. She was thinking I was making her dreary wedding banquet all the better. Wasn't she?"

"I don't know what kind of dull affair it would have been if you hadn't come along," he conceded. Tom was trying to leave the room, but he just couldn't. "Everyone was in disarray when you walked in." He chuckled. "Utter disarray."

I sighed. "It was fun until it wasn't. I've never seen so many cameras, you know. All those peepers." I closed my eyes, maybe to forget, but it was going to be hard to forget a man like Mr. Andino.

Tom bowed. "We'll get this all straightened out. I imagine you had a room but someone missed their cue. Am I right?"

I looked at him, questioning it all. "I don't know where I lost my shoes."

Tom blushed. "You're not at that ball, Miss." He pointed to the shoes, now forgotten, on the floor. "You're here. With me."

I slid the chiffon down over my shoulders, my waist, my narrow hips, and pulled it out from under the quilt. I flung it aside.

"Please," he chirped. "Mind the rules. I don't think we should be in here."

I popped my head out from under the quilt. "But you brought me here."

His voice rose an octave. "I brought you here to wait. So please, Miss. Please wait." Tom turned off the electric lamp, looked uneasily down the hall, and then pulled the heavy door closed behind him. I heard the key turn in the lock.

I unsnapped the hose from the garters and tore off the corset Mrs. Harrison had insisted I wear. I leapt off the bed and onto the pink wool roses, but I was careful not to step on the thorns. I stepped into the bathroom and squatted on the porcelain toilet. There was blood in my bloomers and now it was in the water. It was my blood, and it came from my body, but I stared at it none-theless, alarmed. I knew what men did to girls, what happened when they had relations, for hadn't I heard Ma and Pa go at it enough times, but I never knew there would be this. I should have said no, I shuddered, when Mr. Andino first pulled me across the dance floor thinking I was someone else and making everyone else think it too. I touched my leg where his hand had lingered, where his fingers had teased, where his eyes had burrowed. I should have said no when he fed me that line.

I burped up the taste of last night's salmon mousse and kicked the soiled bloomers under the tub. "Such an idiot," I thought, pulling on the white porcelain handle. Clean water from the tank swirled into the bowl taking the blood with it. I imagined it going where the rest of the rats live. In the sewer. "What was I thinking?" I wailed, "letting Mr. Andino put me in that part? A starlet! How crass." I would have to speak to him. He would need to make things right. After all, this was all on him. Wasn't it? He was the one who made me out to be someone I'm not.

Immediately, there was a knock on the door. I threw a towel around my body and tiptoed across the room. "Tom? Is that you?" I called.

I heard a high-pitched voice from behind the door. "The *Times*, Miss."

"I don't look at the papers, Tom. They're rubbish." Slowly, a "Social Notes" page slipped in from under the door. I knocked anxiously. "Tom? Is that you?"

"Yes, Miss," he squeaked.

"What happened to your voice?"

"Look at the paper, Miss. While you wait." There was a pause. "I'll see to it you're well attended to."

"Maybe you'll bring me a cup of gin. I have a crashing headache." There was more silence. "Are you there, Tom? Unlock the door, Tom," I called, rattling the knob. "Where are you?" I listened at the door until I heard only the patter of his feet on the carpeted floor as he hurried away.

"What a piece of dry toast," I complained. "No butter. Nothing." I left the newspaper, untouched, on the apartment floor and scurried back to the comfort of my bathroom. The water came out hot immediately from the faucet, unlike anything I had ever seen before, and I filled the white porcelain tub with geranium oil. Off came Ma's cotton slip and brassiere.

I stared at the water as it swirled about. Willing the spinning to stop, I put a hand to my forehead. I should have said *no* when I was lobbed back and forth like a shuttlecock for last night's peepers, I thought, chastising myself. I should have said *no* and meant it. Suddenly, I felt more naked than I had ever felt before. I stared at my reflection in the fragrant water as the thought of what I had done began to cut into me. I was a fool to come upstairs with a strange man. "Good girls don't do that. Do they?"

I turned and looked into the mirror. "Do they, Mrs. H.? That's not what happens in *The Blue Book*."

I eased myself down into the hot water and looked at the dried bloodstains between my legs. I thought how easy it would be to lose myself in here. I could slip my head under the water and never wake up. I would never go back to my mother's one-room apartment or trudge down the hall to that rusted old bath ridden with lice. There would be no more Mrs. Harrison's prying eyes on me, no demanding posture, no grammar, no exacting novels. No more Greek tragedies, no imported teas, no lace doilies, and no overfed Charlie. I would never return to myself.

The blood began to loosen from my ivory skin and darken the water. I sank further down into the bath and let the blood and the oil mix together as I ran my hands through the water washing the scent of Mr. Andino off of me. I was fondled, I thought, pouring more oil over the top of my head and slipping down into the bath until only my face was exposed. Sliding down even further, I held my breath and lay as still as I could on the bottom of the tub. I opened my eyes under the water, but the oil stung so I closed them again. I didn't count time like Mrs. Harrison taught me to count time on the dance floor, 1-2-3-4, 1-2-3-4, but I continued to count all the times I should have said *no* to Mr. Andino. I should have said *no* when he first locked eyes with me, when he tapped Charlie's shoulder on the dance floor with his immaculate white-gloved hand, and when he took a step toward me in a pair of polished black slippers as he maneuvered that confident hand onto my back. I should have said *no* when Mr. Andino, dressed in a white tie and black tails, deftly helped me recover from a missed dance step as he pulled me across the dance floor and away from Charlie's nervous laughter.

<>

"Are you the heiress everyone is talking about?" he asked. "I saw you earlier while passing the confectionary." The gentleman raised a dark eyebrow. "Sipping sodas with a fan?" he asked. "And now you're here, the belle of the ball." He grinned and, with ease, turned me on the dance floor. "You must have been quite flattered to have been invited. And to this, the wedding of the season." He looked about the vaulted room, and with a wave of one hand addressed the two rows of crimson box seats above us. Both the leering gentlemen and the gawking women stood up from their chairs and clapped as we passed. All about the cathedral-like room the wedding guests leaned in. Peering over their plates of Beef Wellington and buttered peas, served to them on white hotel china, they smiled coyly and raised their eyes to me. They whispered. Some even lay their hands on the white tablecloths. In unison, they lifted their crystal glasses and cheered.

"Obviously, the Mr. and Mrs. Wayland Townsend are quite undone by it all," the distinguished man continued. He looked on me approvingly as he led me in a waltz. "Dressing things up for them, aren't you? Cutting the rug." I looked up into his mud-colored eyes and smiled bashfully. With a vitality I was unaccustomed to, he turned me once more, and this time I couldn't help but swoon. No one I knew, not even Mrs. Harrison, could dance like this. We glided across the parquet floor while everyone, including the bride and her groom, stepped out of the way. "Are you staying with us?" he continued, with a wave of his hand toward the ivory friezes decorating the walls. The room was outfitted with so much marble I felt like I had been transported to the isles of Greece.

"Must feel good to be back on these familiar streets, doesn't it?" he offered. I smiled nervously. My yellow chiffon spun about the room as the many eyes followed. From the painted ceiling, a band of frolicking, half-dressed nymphs looked down on us. The gentleman smiled and looked down at my new shoes approvingly. "If you would do me the honor of parading with me down Peacock Alley," he said, referring to the fashionable corridor connecting the Waldorf and the Astoria buildings, "I will..."

I looked up with uncertainty. "You will do what, Sir?"

He managed a grin. "Please don't call me Sir. Makes me feel old. To you, let it be Lawrence."

"You're not old," I said to please him.

Lawrence smiled broadly while his narrow black mustache made only the slightest motion on his upper lip. "I'm not as young as I once was," he explained. He offered me the crook of his arm where I was expected to place my own as he escorted me off the dance floor. I couldn't help but notice the way the fashionable men, dressed in their black tie and tails, and the gilded women weighed down by diamonds, genuflected. The room was so heavy with the weight of their money I nearly sank to my knees right then and there. Lawrence took me by the elbow and through the ballroom doors as the crowd leaned in to get a better view.

"You're the envy," he explained. "Even that stodgy bride, Madeline," he whistled, "is wishing she wore lemon chiffon to her wedding banquet. Never in my life have I seen such fun." I winced. "Never before have I had this much pleasure. You really do know how to get a Prohibition party up and running." I turned to look for Charlie, but he was nowhere to be found in the midst of the crowded revelry. "I'll bring you back to him," said Lawrence. "You'll do me such an honor. Walking with me. With me..."

"Me?"

"I envy women," he explained. "Such folly."

"I'm just a girl," I offered. "But I know a thing or two about folly. My pa..."

Lawrence continued to look down at me and smiled broadly as we took a turn together on the stairs. He wasn't listening. "Are you back in Manhattan shooting a new picture?"

"A picture?" I asked, genuinely confused.

"And now all the way up here in this rain."

"Oh, I don't mind the rain," I exclaimed. "This is the most exciting night of my life. Being here." He lifted his hand inviting me to put my gloved hand on the back of his as he escorted me down the wide marbled steps.

"I'm flattered," said Lawrence.

"You are?"

Lawrence grinned. "It's not every day I can say I've seen such a woman." I blushed. "No one told us you'd be here. Imagine! Here at the Waldorf-Astoria. Even the groom seems astounded. Quite taken with you, you know." He kept churning out the compliments and I smiled. "Did you know what fun you'd be?

What fun you'd bring to that gnosis-inspired tomb?" I felt certain he was referring to the ballroom and I shook my head. "Things have certainly dried up for us, you know. Confections?" he complained, chiding the candy counter. "Makes for a dull party, doesn't it?" I looked up at his rakish smile. "We had some raucous times in that old bourbon bar." He laughed quietly to himself. "But they tore it out of here and auctioned it off piece by piece. Life sure was fun before those damned senators came along." His eyes, dark pools of liquid, oozed like oil onto me. He was looking for an answer. "I am quite fond of a Rob Roy," he explained.

"I like licorice drops," I trilled.

He grinned. "You would, wouldn't you?"

I turned to look up at him. "I would?"

"You just seem like the kind of woman to like something difficult to chew." Lawrence laughed louder. "You will get noticed down here too, you know," he said, as we took a step into the bustling columned corridor. "I don't doubt there will be a bit of a hullabaloo, but you're used to that, aren't you?"

"I'm not sure I understand."

"Your shoes," he continued, taking a step so that all who saw me waltzing on his arm down the long wide corridor could turn and look, "are avant-garde. Did you know you would be bringing us such a fashion? Such a fashion," he said, repeating himself. I looked down at the party shoes. They were practically bursting at the seams they were so tight. I wanted to tell him that the shoes were nothing special, antiques, long ago discarded and left to rot on a dime-store shelf.

Lawrence took a turn with me as we walked down one side of the marbled-lined corridor and back up the other. True to his word, all eyes were on me, on the shoes, and on the lemon chiffon. I tiptoed over the carpets nervously, then turned to him and sang, "I've never been in a parade before."

He looked down onto me, incredulously, and grinned. "Of course you've been on parade. Next time I will find you a gold carpet to step upon." I looked down at my feet then turned my eyes upward to explore the pink marbled columns that went all the way to the dark coffered ceiling. Lawrence smiled curiously. "Maybe red," he offered. "I'll see to it that next time you're on parade, you're parading on something fit for a queen."

I pulled away in alarm. "Red? Are you so brazen that you would take me to my death?"

Lawrence pulled in his chin, puckered his lips, and laughed. "You are quite the actress, aren't you?"

"I never thought of myself as an actress, but I have been in several of Mrs. Harrison's Greek stories. Her tableaux. I know about the blood. The spoils of war," I explained, pointing to the carpets. "Of death."

He chuckled. "Come now. Surely you can do better than that."

I turned on my heels and took a step away from him. "I haven't much," I offered, "but I do have a modern education. Mrs. Harrison," I said, determined to set him straight, "sees to it. She is my tutor. I'm not some frivolity. I do things. I make things. I...what I'm trying to say is I can do more than act. I can do more than perform steps."

"I understand," he said gravely. "What then does that make me?" Alarmed, I looked up at him, but he took me by the elbow, playfully, and fondled the ends of Mrs. Harrison's long white glove with his own. "You're so petite," he purred, leaning down and whispering in my ear. Maybe that was his tongue tickling me. "I thought you would be taller."

"I need to go," I said, pulling away from him, but he tightened his grip on my elbow. His gloves were much cleaner than Charlie's, which had become stained with perspiration. There were both high hats and impeccably dressed women with their baubles watching us from the sidelines. They sat gawking on the cracked leather chairs that lined the corridor. I couldn't escape. Their hungry gaze followed us with each step I took, and with a nod of their overdressed heads, they smiled.

I pushed at the gloves and peeled them down my trembling hands. "Here," I said frantically, "keep these as a reminder of our parade. I must get back to....to my date."

"I'm honored," said Lawrence bowing. He waved the gloves in the air so the rest of the arena could see. It was as if he had won some conquest. And do you know what those peepers did? They clapped.

I think I ran all the way back up the grand stairs and down the hall to the ballroom where I remember throwing myself, in terror, against the doors.

<>

"This is all Charlie's fault," I hissed, sitting up in the bath and gagging. I spit up the geranium-scented water and cried. "None of this is my fault."

V

When Charlie was ten years old I watched him, from the studio dance floor, touch himself. I didn't know then that what he was doing was called fondling, only that his pudgy hands were on his pants while his eyes, wide, seemed locked on me. I looked at him, curiously, but Mrs. Harrison swept him out of the room with the kind of ferocity you see when men move their pigs out of the street and into a waiting pen. Mrs. Harrison was pushing at him, prodding, while I stood alone in the middle of a polished floor waiting for "Dapper Dan" to play on the phonograph. When Mrs. Harrison returned to the dance floor, took my hands in hers, and reprimanded me sharply for toddling, she never told me that Charlie was only doing what boys do. I only learned about it last night.

I stood in front of the bathroom mirror, naked, remembering the first time I saw Charlie touch himself. I was twelve years old, narrow and unusually small for my age. I was wearing a pair of Charlie's old riding jodhpurs, because at the time, Ma was often given his hand-me-downs in exchange for her work. Cash was rarely exchanged in the early days, and so whatever Mrs. Harrison had on hand she gave to Ma, who took the clothes and boots and passed them on to me. I didn't wear a frock until I was thirteen.

When Ma first went to work for the Harrisons she had insisted I was old enough to contribute to our family's welfare so she would bring me along. I was only a child then, and I would help her sweep the floor and pick up cigarette butts, but one day when Mrs. Harrison saw me on my hands and knees scrubbing away black shoe polish she told my mother, in that opulent angry voice of hers, that Ma was irresponsible to force floor cleaning on a six-year-old child. And so in those lazy long days when Ma worked for more than one needing soul while Pa peddled a taffy cart on the pocked streets of Manhattan, I sat in the doorway of Mrs. Harrison's dance studio and replayed her dancing steps over and over in my mind.

Ma and I knew Pa's taffy was stolen, although we kept our mouths shut. We had enough on our minds then. I had some kind of talent Mrs. Harrison saw as natural in the way I memorized her dance steps quickly, and with ease. While Pa filled his coat pockets with contraband, Mrs. Harrison swept up the missing pieces of my life and introduced me to the foxtrot, to grammar, to literature, to radio dramas, to the phonograph, to dressmaking, to desire. And when I turned thirteen, and Pa was still out looking for his due, Mrs. Harrison thought it high time I owned a frock. I remember she took me by the arm and carted me down the bustling sidewalks to a set of tall revolving doors. When those glass doors spun around and brought me inside, I took one delirious look at what lay beyond. I remember Mrs. Harrison looked down at me then and smiled. She was delighted. Finally, she could "bring me up to speed," she said, by introducing me to this unexplored exotic world. This was not the five-and-dime where women clomped about in broken brogues. This was Macy's where I would be exchanging one fraying red awning for a bright red one that waved triumphantly.

I'll never forget that first step I took beyond those moving doors. With the kind of determination one gets when one sees something unimagined, imagined, I placed one of Charlie's old battered boots, which was scuffed, unlike most of the ladies' pumps going in and out of there, down onto the old wooden floor. Over-lit, as if from faerie dust, the store seemed ready to explode, magically, from within. So taken was I by the sight and smell of all that was new, I simply reached out my hand and chose the first frock I saw. Of course Mrs. Harrison objected, thinking I should spend more time in Macy's, get to know the fashions, "the lay of the land," as she called it, before committing to the frock, but I knew what I wanted the minute I saw it and nothing she could do to persuade me otherwise would suit. My mind was made up.

Mrs. Harrison took the navy-blue-and-white polka dot frock with its three tiers of fabric and long navy waist tie to the sales counter and asked a young woman dressed in a fashionable grey suit if she would kindly wrap it for her. The delighted woman beamed.

"You've chosen well," she said, eyeing me. "You'll no doubt be the talk of the town." Mrs. Harrison frowned. "In no time," she added playfully. I peered up at her from where I stood on the tips of my toes behind the glass counter. I remember looking into her tussled auburn curls and thinking I wanted to be where she was on the other side of the counter seeing what she was seeing for me. She shared another smile and asked me where I was going. Embarrassed, I shook my head.

Mrs. Harrison complained. "Dancing," she explained. "That's all Edie does."

The sales clerk nodded, pleased. "Going dancing. Well, you sure do know how to pick them, Edie." She handed Mrs. Harrison a pair of black patent leather Mary Janes with a definitive flick of her jangling gold-bangled wrist. Mrs. Harrison nodded, alarmed. There was going to be no saying no to proper dancing shoes. I watched Mrs. Harrison count her bills, and when she took every last one of them out of her black coin purse and handed them over like she was handing them over to the executioner, Mrs. Harrison paused and looked down at me. "You're going places, Miss Edith May. No one spends this kind of money on something so frivolous unless they know where they're going."

I still think about that frock. I wore it every day until the seams burst and I could no longer stuff my still-growing body into it. When Mrs. Harrison chose the lemon chiffon for my birthday party at the Waldorf-Astoria candy counter, I know she did so without consulting me because she was afraid I might, once again, find the most expensive one in all of Macy's. I keep that frock under my crib in a piece of discolored tissue paper, the kind of thin paper that only the Mrs. Harrisons of this world could have in their possession.

I would have to have a way forward, she explained when she first dressed me in that navy-blue-and-white polka dot number. She shooed my mother's prying eyes away from the discussion, but Ma must have been looking and learning. When Ma spied those expensive dancing shoes on the top shelf of the five-and-dime, I think it was her way of giving me back what I had long been missing.

<>

I pulled my oil-soaked hair away from my face, sat down on the edge of the tub, and wept. My hair was ruined. I was ruined. How would Mr. Andino see me now? "Curse you, Edie," I cringed. "Can't you do anything right?" I yanked on my limp hair and cried harder. If only I could step back into that little girl's frock were I once felt safe, where I was once honored, and where I once gave Mrs. Harrison hope.

"Edie," she used to say to me, "you just got born, like so many children, on the crack in the sidewalk. That's all. Some people get the chasms that mark their life while others do the repairing. I, for one, will repair your chasm," she promised me. I never understood what she meant by this, not then. But I was beginning to understand it now.

I gave the dirty bathwater a deliberate slap. I thought about slipping back down into the tub and filling my lungs with the blood, with Mr. Andino's scent, and with the greasy residue of the Madame's sickly sweet geranium oil. "Idiot," I shrieked. "How did I get here?" It felt good to cry. At last. I had held it inside for too long. "I'm such a knob," I thought. "A stupid knob." My face was blotchy from the sleepless night and my curls were ruined. My hair hung limply to my shoulders for the pins had been lost, I'm certain, somewhere in Mr. Andino's bed. "Curses," I hissed. "I can't go to him like this." I wrapped myself up in the

Madame's pink silk robe and tucked my hair, turban-like, into one of her clean white towels. "Curse you, Charlie," I winced. "You should have fought for me."

There was a knock on the apartment door. Startled, I called out, "Tom?"

"No," he said sarcastically, while fitting the key into the lock and swinging the door open. "Dracula." He took a step back when he saw me and cried, "Mother Mary."

"Don't use her name that way," I tried. I looked him over carefully up and down. "Where's my gin?"

"Are you outta your mind, Miss?" he cried, nearly dropping to his knees. "What did you go and do to yourself?"

"Oh shut up," I said, frantically searching the Madame's private writing desk, "and help me find a pair of scissors."

He cringed. "What for?"

I pulled off the towel to show him the lifeless hair. He took a step back and choked, "Mr. Andino's not gonna recognize you."

"Mr. Andino won't be seeing me like this," I insisted, pulling out a wad of the Madame's thick ivory correspondence cards and tossing it aside.

Tom walked all over the thorns on the carpet as if he had nothing to be afraid of. When he crossed into the room I noticed that he had polished his dark boots. He wouldn't take his eyes off me. "What happened to your curls?"

I turned away from him and continued rummaging through the desk drawer. "Help me, Tom," I pleaded. "I've got to cut it."

Tom took a step backwards and shook his head. "I gotta get you out of here, Miss," he rebuked. He pulled on the Madame's imposing wardrobe doors and plucked a wooden box of contraband liquor out from behind the fur sleeves. "What I wouldn't give for a thumbnail of gin myself," he said, inhaling deeply and unlocking the box. He poured a drop of gin into a glass and handed it to me. "One sip. Just one. And then we leave. Mr. Andino's agreed to a breakfast."

"A breakfast?" I wailed, tipping back the gin. "I can't have a breakfast." I choked on the astringent taste of the bootleg liquor. "Not like this. Not now."

"You said you wanted..."

"I know what I said, but that was before..." I croaked, pulling out a pair of silver filigree scissors from the back of the desk drawer and pointing them to my hair.

"Oh no you're not," cried Tom, reaching for the scissors. "You're mad. And you're gonna get me bumped."

"Look at me, Tom," I insisted, securing the scissors in my hand. "For the first time in my life I feel something. I feel it. And it's good." Tom looked at me, aghast. "Cut it," I pleaded, pushing the scissors onto him. "Please, Tom. Do this for me."

His eyes went wide. "I don't know you, Miss. I can't just take a pair of scissors to your hair. Your beautiful curls," he bemoaned. I sensed that he was searching my face as if he was still looking for them. "I don't understand. What happened?"

"I don't know, Tom, but I want it off. All of it. Just like Irene Castle. I want to look like her."

"But you need to look like you."

"I will."

He was reprimanding. "No self-respectin' woman cuts her hair."

"And who made you such a bluenose? Cut it, Tom. Or else I scream."

"I won't," he said, backing away. "I came to fetch you. And you need to be fetched. Please. Get dressed, Miss. Now."

"Limp toast," I cried, pulling the bathroom door closed and locking it.

Tom rapped his gloved knuckles on the door. "Better than being a cake-eater. Got *that*? I could have told you Mr. Andino was no good, but you're the one who fell for it. And now you're payin' the price and blamin' me. Well, don't blame me. I came to you offerin' help. I genuinely thought you were her. We all did. Well?" he shouted, rapping loudly on the bathroom door. "Are you or are you not?"

There was a long silence and then I heard him sit down, heavily, on the bed. I wielded the scissors in one hand and yanked open the bathroom door with the other. I crossed the room, careful to avoid the thorns, and pointed the scissors directly at Tom's heart.

I hissed. "Get off my bed."

He shot up. "You're crazy."

"You're vulgar. Sitting on my bed."

"Look," Tom squealed, leaping off the bed. "I thought I was doin' you a favor bringin' you up here and away from every Sunday mornin' gawker." His knees buckled as if he was about to go soft. "Crumpled up on that uncomfortable old sofa as if you'd spent the whole night there. And I thought...well, I know you don't want your name in the papers, Miss Ayres. Not like that."

"You think I'm a starlet from the motion pictures. Is that it?"

Tom shook his head, embarrassed. "Well, maybe I am. Maybe

I've got you fooled. Ever think of that? Ever think maybe I'm rehearsing a new picture and I've got you in my sights for the leading man? Imagine that."

"Liar!" he balked.

"Then cut my hair."

Tom looked me over carefully. "You're not really a starlet, are you?"

"I don't know what I am!" I shrieked.

"We all thought it. From the minute you took that runnin' leap into Mr. Andino's waitin' arms. We knew it."

I wailed. "I didn't take a running leap. He just pulled me away while I was dancing with Charlie. He took me away with him."

Tom put his hands on his hips and smiled, remembering. "You sure took a shine to that ballroom. All those partners. You in those glad rags. High-steppin' it in those fancy shoes. I knew it then."

"Knew what?" I cried.

His eyes widened. "Looky what I won," he said, pulling a crumpled five-dollar bill out of his pocket. "More money than I could have ever won playin' poker. And all because I said who you were. And then when you were chosen, over all those other beauties, they knew it too."

I grimaced. "Who knew what? Gad. You are annoying."

"But I won the bet," he said, pocketing the money. "A whole fin." He looked at me and in all seriousness said, "It was the shoes that gave you away."

I swung around. "I hate those shoes, Tom. Got that? I hate them. If it wasn't for those shoes I wouldn't be here." He looked at me, expressionless. "I hate my hair and I want it cut. If you don't cut it I will. And then I will walk into Mr. Andino's room and demand he make things right."

Tom took a step away from me. "You can't make things right with a man like Mr. Andino. He's a Tycoon." Tom crossed the floor and poured himself a swallow of gin. "Do you know what a Tycoon does?" he asked, draining the glass. I lifted a sodden curl and lopped it off. "Miss," Tom exclaimed, "you can't do that!"

"I've been compromised and it's all your fault."

"My fault?" he shouted, reaching for the scissors.

"Thinking I was a starlet from the motion pictures. Thinking I needed rescuing. Thinking for me." I grabbed his arm and pinned it behind his back. "I didn't need to come up here, Tom. I was going to go home and forget this birthday ever happened. Charlie is a child and I never should have been allowed to come here with him. Mrs. Harrison was a fool to send me here unchaperoned." I released his arm and pulled away from him. "She was thinking for me. That I needed more educating. That this posh hotel," I offered, indicating the Madame's imported tile fireplace and Chinese lacquer screen, "was somehow something better." I turned from Tom and put my hands to my heart. "I walked right onto a Titanic," I cursed. "I never thought Mr. Andino..."

Tom turned anxiously and looked at the apartment door. "You've got it all wrong, Miss. Mr. Harrison is not a child. He's goin' places."

I howled. "Going where? Into the ballroom dance business? He's not going anywhere. Not if he keeps eating his way through all those confections. No. My ma was using me," I complained, lifting another one of my sodden curls and chopping it off. "She was using me to get herself out of that two-bit life of hers. Well, you know what," I shouted, shooting him a look of disgust. "I don't want that two-bit life either, but I sure as hell don't want this." I laughed cruelly. "Look at this place. Gad. It's crawling with ghosts. Ghosts in the carpets. Ghosts in the brass bed. Ghosts in the gilded frames, the cracked wallpapers, and in all these ugly urns."

"These are Italian antiques," said Tom defensively.

I pointed the scissors at all the fussy foreign objects in the room. "Stolen works of pretentious art."

Tom was adamant. "We're the finest."

I balked. "At deceiving."

Tom was dejected, I could tell, but I wasn't about to tell him the whole story, that of my pa and his "wanderings," as Ma called them. If Pa wasn't the man we knew him to be, I might forgive him for all that he's done to us, leaving us so that he could become the hero of his own cowboy reel, but I can't forgive a man who thinks he's somehow better out on the open road and not at home. I threw Tom a look of genuine concern. "No, you wouldn't know about deceiving, would you?" I said softening. "Only one day you'll learn it just like all the men I've ever known." I clipped another one of the curls and my dark brown hair fell to the floor.

"I'm sorry, Miss," said Tom, picking up the fallen curls. "I mean it. I am sorry if you were deceived, but that's on you..."

"No, that's on you," I tried. "You had no business coming to help me. None at all."

"But..."

"Cut it, Tom. I hate it."

"There's nothin' I want more than for you to be happy, Miss Ayres, but I haven't sorted this out. If I don't do right, and you go back to Paramount with..."

"Oh my god, Tom. I'm me. Don't you get it?"

He looked down at me as if studying me, questioning me, or rather questioning himself. I could see the wheels turn. Finally, he relaxed and the corners of his mouth turned up into a wide grin. "Game up, Miss Ayres," he laughed, throwing his hands to the ceiling in defeat. "You win. That's the best performance I've seen you do. Get dressed. I'll get you a pair of cheaters and we can get you out of here. No one will ever know you've been up here. And I'm not invested in your story. I can keep a secret."

I pulled him into me. "Get me another thumbnail of gin, Tom. And cut my hair."

VI

"It's smart," Tom offered, obviously pleased with the results. "Really. You look swell."

I twisted a wet curl around my finger and pinned it. Tom pilfered more pins from the back of the vanity drawer and gave them to me. "I have to hand it to you, Miss Ayres, you do modern well. Better than Irene Castle. Better than most. Better than I ..."

"You have no idea what I'm capable of, Tom," I said, handing him the empty glass. The gin was good. The more I drank, the more I liked it.

Tom grinned. "Now I know what you're capable of. You're capable of this," he said, indicating the mess of lopped-off curls in the bathroom sink.

I looked at myself in the opulent mirror and smiled. I liked what I saw. I think I was searching for Irene. Maybe? Wasn't I? I extended one lean leg, pointed my toe on the black-and-white tiled floor, and lifted my arms to the ceiling imitating one of her dancing moves I'd seen in a photograph. I knew I wasn't the girl I was last night and I turned to Tom to explain. "I can't go to Mr. Andino in last night's party frock."

He stumbled out of the bathroom. "No?"

"Please, Tom. Find me a new frock. Anything," I begged, following him. "Mr. Andino can't know he won. Got that? I can't go to him and let him think of me as last night's goods. I have integrity, you know." Tom looked stricken. "I mean it."

He scanned the Madame's imposing tangerine wardrobe. It stood out in the room like a fierce warrior outfitted with the kind of highfalutin weaponry one would need to do battle downstairs in Peacock Alley, where all the fashionable men and women come to gawk and be gawked at. "You want me to steal for you?"

I waved my hand to dismiss him. "The Madame is fat. I've already gone through her clothes. I can't wear a thing."

Tom nodded. "I don't imagine you want an antique now that you've cut your hair."

"Precisely," I trilled. "Look in your newspapers, Tom. What are the Moderns wearing?"

"You're in the epicenter of modern," said Tom brightly, "in Hollywood. You don't need us."

"Oh, but I do. I need knowledge. 'The more we learn the better we discern.' " I looked up at Tom and smiled. "I made that up, you know."

"Well, make up something else," he suggested. "Some new style. And then take it back to California."

"I'm not going to California, Tom. I'm going..." I shot him a look of uncertainty. "I don't know where I'm going."

Tom smiled. "Doesn't matter. You're goin' straight to the top, Miss Ayres. I feel it."

I laughed. "Do you, Tom? Do you really feel it? I think I know what you mean." I pushed another pin into my hair and tucked a curl behind my ear.

Tom hesitated and then returned to the bathroom with a fireplace broom to sweep up the fallen hair. "I'll tell Mr. Andino that you've been detained while I find you a new frock."

"No. That won't do. He won't wait for me. And why should he? You said so yourself. He's a very important man." I looked at Tom, carefully. "Is he? Really? Or is that just another one of your lines?"

"What do you mean?"

"I mean do you even know who Mr. Andino really is? What he does?"

"I told you. He's a Tycoon."

I shook my head. "You don't know, do you?"

"I do."

"Well, whatever he is he's not going to wait for me. I need a new frock and shoes pronto," I explained. "Now."

"I want to do right, but..."

"All you have to do," I suggested, "is run over to Macy's and..."

Tom frowned. "I have a job. I serve others, you know. Not just you. The whole rest of the floor. I have..."

"It's one favor, Tom. One. Here, put your arms around my waist," I said, lifting his hands and putting them around the Madame's loose-fitting robe, "to get an idea of my size." His hands were damp and if he wasn't so frightened I think I could have kissed him. His lips were chapped but plump. They were not thin like my father's or hidden behind a narrow wax mustache. He looked at me, alarmed. "There. Got that?" I said, reluctantly pulling my eyes away from his cobalt gems. "And take the shoes with you. Get me something daring. Something no one else will have. Something..." I insisted, looking down at my feet and thinking of the word. "Avant-garde. It's what he will expect."

Tom stepped away. "You want me to steal goods for you? I can't do that, Miss Ayres."

"No, you cad. Charge it. Charge it to Mrs. Harrison. No," I screeched. "Better yet, charge it to Mr. Andino. Oh, and get me a hat," I begged. "Please, Tom. And silk stockings."

"You can't do this, Miss Ayres. It's not right."

"It's not right that Charlie," I said remembering, "left me alone with a creeper old enough to be my father! I deserve it."

"I don't know..."

"Of course you do, Tom. You know I'm eager just as you are. We're eager to do right by this world, aren't we?" Tom nodded. "We just don't have a leg up. That's all. You're looking for a leg up and now you have money in your pocket to prove it. Who gets your fin, Tom? Your ma or your pa?"

He looked at me, uncertain. "I keep it, Miss Ayres. Me."

"Your pa won't take it from you?"

Tom softened. "My pa died." I looked down at the floor. "And my ma won't be needin' it. She's gone too."

I took a step into him and tightened the silk robe as it began to slip off my shoulders. "Golly, Tom. Why didn't you say?" He shrugged. "You got nothing then. No one?"

"Just my sis," he said, looking across the room at the rejected dancing shoes. "My pa was a..." He hesitated.

"I bet he was a good man," I offered. "Just like you."

Tom grimaced. "A wrong number."

I studied him. "Did he ever hurt your sister?" Tom didn't answer. He dropped my fallen curls into the toilet, and without thinking, pulled on the handle. I watched as the lopped-off pieces of myself drained away. Frightened, I turned to the mirror, but I liked what I saw and I smiled.

"One favor. Just one," he said, exiting the bathroom. "But you need B. Altman, Miss Ayres. That's where you'll find what you're lookin' for."

I followed Tom out of the bathroom, looked up at him, and smiled. "Whatever you say, Tom."

"And then you must leave us. Unless of course you'd like me to get you a room. Which I can do. I'm sure we have better suites that would suit. You can charge it to the studio," he suggested, sweeping his hands over the outdated, overly dressed room, "then you can stay as long as you'd like."

"No. No, I need to be getting on," I stammered. "Take the shoes, Tom, and get me a larger size." I smiled. "Please."

Tom looked down at the soiled shoes. He placed a hand on his heart then turned and studied the door. With fanfare, he turned again and curled his fingers over the dancing shoes as if extracting them from some previous life. He grinned. "You don't want them?" I shook my head, *no*.

Tom closed the door behind him, this time leaving it unlocked. I let the robe fall to the floor, where it lay in a pool of discarded silk. I crawled back into the bed to wait for him, my mind on what I would say to Mr. Andino, and what, if anything, I should ask for. I could ask for reparation, for an apology. I could serve him with a cruel promise that should I ever get my sights on the certain kinds of individuals who might take a man out for the crimes he's committed against women, I could send them here to the Waldorf-Astoria Hotel. I could threaten Mr. Andino with death, with ruin. I could extort him or bribe him. My head raced through every motion picture scene, the plots of novels, the Greek myths, and the radio plays. I knew words, deeds, and motives, but somehow this story felt different. This was real. I wasn't starring in a motion picture or a Greek tragedy. I was in my life, and yet somehow this wasn't turning out to be my life. It was turning into a farce.

I closed my eyes, for how long I don't know, when suddenly there was a sharp knock on the door and I sat up, disconcerted and disoriented. I reached out thinking that I would grab the sides of my crib, but when I stretched, I touched nothing. "Coming," I managed. This wasn't our apartment. It was a darkened room, and the light from behind an ivory scrim came through the veil in thin parallel lines. I looked at the light lines stretching over the patterned carpets. My head spun. I was hungry, I realized, and my mouth was parched. I lifted my head from the eiderdown and looked around, allowing my eyes to adjust to the dim light.

"Miss Ayres," came an urgent voice from behind the closed door. "May I?"

"I'm coming," I managed sleepily. "Who is it?"

"Miss Agnes Ayres," sang a confident female voice. "I've brought ya yar travelin' things."

I pulled the robe off the floor and reached for the knob. When I turned it I did so without pause, but I was uncertain. "Traveling?" I asked, opening the door.

A big-bosomed woman in grey flannel, a seamstress of sorts, or so I thought, came through the door, and with a quick unapologetic gesture flicked on the electric candle lamps. The room was awash in a golden glow and I adjusted my eyes once more. I saw that her hair was pulled tight to her head in a high topknot. She wore sturdy round-toed work shoes and had a commanding presence about her, not unlike Mrs. Harrison. I took another nervous glance at her. She wore a red velvet corsage of dressmaking pins on her wrist and waddled as she walked across the room. The middle-aged woman dropped a pile of white boxes on one of the mahogany tables, and with the ease of a one-armed rodeo cowboy moved a tall arrangement of white Casablanca lilies across the table to make room for it all.

"I'll change those out for orchids, Miss Ayres," she said easily. "That's more the fashion." Her jaunty voice rose and fell just like one of the many foreign lilts I had heard all my life. I looked up expecting to see one of the noisy trains banging along on the elevated. "Just as we'll freshen ya up." She smiled. I watched her advance across the floor with ease. She opened the thin curtains and then turned at last to look at me. "I was summoned," she said bowing, "to come to yar aid." I nodded uneasily. "Do ya know they opened the store for ya? For ya?" she said grinning.

I swallowed hard. "For me? No!"

"I have the loveliest dove grey travelin' frock for ya, Miss Ayres." She opened a crisp white box with an elaborate scrolling BA on the lid with an apparent flair for showing off.

I wracked my brain for just what to say. "First, she has me all wrong," I thought. "I don't look good in grey. And secondly, where exactly am I going?"

"Ya will adore this," she sang. "I picked it out myself. Personally. Mr. Andino gave me instructions. He said and I quote: 'No limits.'" She hugged the frock and matching dove grey coat, loaded down with a mink fur collar and cuffs, to her chest. "Can ya imagine that? No limits!"

I studied her wide-set eyes. It was as though she was asking for a response. I couldn't help but notice how the grey hair at her temples stood out, sentry-like, from the rest of the dark hair on her forehead. "How did you know my size?" I winced.

"Oh, that's easy," she said, continuing to eye me, jauntily. She turned the traveling coat inside out, studied the handiwork, and then looked to me again. She ran her hands over the dark brown fur and purred. "Take out yar hairpins, Miss Ayres. Ya won't be needin' to curl yar hair. Now that…well, now that ya've gone an' cut it."

I threw my hands to my hair. I had forgotten what I had done. "It was the gin," I said weakly.

"Nah. It was all ya," she offered. "Girls will take one look at ya and wanna be like ya. Ya'll be the talk of the town." She reached toward me, as if without thinking, and adjusted the strays. With a swift eager hand she swept all but one of the dark curls off my forehead. "We'll put some wave here," she suggested, tucking the rest of my bobbed hair behind my ear.

"Oh, but that goes against…what I mean to say is, I'm not…"

"Ya're being too modest, Miss Ayres. Come now. Give me 'em pins. Ya did a masterful job with the bob. Masterful," she admitted, complimenting Tom's haircut.

"I had help," I offered. "I didn't do the lines."

She lifted my chin with her outstretched hand and traced her calloused fingers along my jaw. "Ya have excellent lines. Good bone structure too. I brought ya some lipstick."

"Lipstick?" I exclaimed. "Mrs. Harrison doesn't approve of lipstick."

The woman laughed and put her hands on her wide hips. "Ya're not in Mrs. Harrison's dressin' room now, are ya, lass?"

I looked at her and smiled weakly. "Are those traveling shoes?" I asked, pointing to another one of the boxes.

With follies flair she opened a pink-and-white striped box of shoes. "My dear, these are the very best that money can buy. Imported from France. 'Charge it to me,' he said. So I did."

The shoes had simple lines, one strap each, elongated toe boxes, and most importantly, they looked like they would fit. I put my hand down on the elegant black leather shoes, the most fashionable shoes on the streets of Paris, according to the seamstress, and cringed. "Mr. Andino really said that?" The wheels had begun to turn in my head. "He knows about all this?" I asked, waving my hand, weakly, over the stack of B. Altman boxes. "And he said, 'Charge it to me'? Mr. Andino?"

She jostled the pins from my hair and continued smoothing out modern spit curls and creating waves by using her thick fingers on my damp hair. "The very one. Our Shippin' Magnate."

I touched my hair, uncertain. "I thought he was a Railroad Tycoon."

"Well, he's somethin'," she conceded, urging me to try on the shoes.

"Something," I repeated uneasily.

"Now don't be gettin' yar knickers in a twist about him. He wanted ya to have silk stockings."

"Silk?"

"And new lingerie," she trilled, opening up more boxes and sifting through the thin papers. "I made sure ya have the garters. An' a bandeau. Although I don't think ya will be needin' the laces to tighten yarself in," she chirped, looking approvingly at my small chest. She opened another box. "A silk slip." And with more flair she pulled open another. "Mr. Andino saw to the French stockings, Miss Ayres. Personally."

I poured myself another thimble of gin and offered her one, but she shook her head. "I don't understand."

"What's thar to understand? Ya have a need and Mr. Andino knew who to call." She blushed. "It shouldn't be me up here, Miss Ayres, but Frances Whiting. Franny, he calls her. She's the personal shopper. She would have been here for ya, but, well, that don't matter now. They came callin' for me, Miss Ayres! Me!"

"Am I a toy?" I asked, pulling on the drink. "A doll?"

"Nah. Nothin' like that, Miss Ayres. We were told ya lost yar luggage. Mr. Andino was comin' to yar aid. We all are. All of us tryin' to do a bit of kindness in this topsy-turvy world."

"Kindness?" I croaked. I knew that if I accepted these expensive Parisian clothes I would lose the trump. "Mr. Andino has outmaneuvered me," I cried, slipping off the robe and crawling back into the bed. "Pull the curtains, Ma'am," I begged. "And take it back. All of it."

VII

Sunlight flooded the room. I cried out fiercely for Tom to close the curtains, but he ignored me. "How could you?" I wailed. "You knew I needed the upper hand."

Tom looked down onto the mahogany table where he had put a silver breakfast tray. He smiled bashfully. "I brought you a continental breakfast, Miss Ayres. Croissant, toast, pastry," he explained. "I thought you might be hungry."

I refused his offer of coffee. "That's the problem with you, Tom. You don't think."

"I couldn't not tell Mr. Andino," he tried. "He and I..."

"You you you," I shouted. "You're only concerned with yourself, Tom. Now look at the mess I'm in."

"You're not in a mess, Miss Ayres. Far from it. This is easily resolved. Perhaps you're just a little down on your luck. That's all. And haven't we all been there before? Aren't we all lookin' for a helpin' hand?"

"You might be, but I'm not."

He smoothed out the creases of his jacket and pulled on it eagerly, once again at the ready. "But you've had help. We've all had help. And now that you're a risin' star, Mr. Andino thought

69

you should look the part. You know. He knows. We all know by the look of things, by your party shoes," he confided, "that you have unrivaled taste."

"My ma," I cursed. "Damn her."

"Now, Miss Ayres. Your ma probably gave you her breast..."

"Oh my god, Tom," I wailed, throwing back the quilt and stepping out of bed. "You're just as crass as I am." He turned when he saw that I was without clothes and busied himself at the breakfast tray.

"Toast?" he croaked.

"Turn around, Tom, and tell me how I'm going to wear those expensive clothes? How?" The traveling frock and matching coat were laid out on the floral chintz sofa next to the silk lingerie, the matching ivory bandeau and slip, the silk stockings, some strange newfangled hat, and the expensive Parisian shoes. I studied it all, alarmed, again, to see the design looking like it belonged on some Hollywood starlet, but not on me.

"Miss, I will leave you to get dressed," said Tom bashfully. "Mr. Andino is waitin' for you in the Palm Room."

I flinched. "The Palm Room?"

"Get dressed, Miss Ayres."

Tom was trying not to get angry, and although he would not turn around to face me, I could hear it in his voice. "I can't be left unchaperoned..."

"Then don't come down to the Waldorf-Astoria, Miss Ayres," he complained, pulling on the door sharply. "We're all about equality here, you know, for the opposite sex. The frail sex isn't so frail in our eyes. Got that? Even our elevator attendants are women. Tell me one other hotel in the whole of Manhattan that hires women for that job?" His voice rose steadily. "Not one. So if you're comin' to the conclusion that you need a...a..." He was getting more and more animated. He hit his fist on the door. "You're playin' into his hands if you refuse him, Miss Ayres. You're a Modern. So be a Modern." Tom slammed the door behind him as he left the room. The electric candle lights flickered and then went out.

"I'm not a Modern," I winced, stuffing a piece of buttered toast into my mouth. I sank to the floor, reached for another piece of toast, and then a third. I swallowed hard. "Damn you, Tom," I squealed. "What a snob." I hit my fist on the table. "I'll tell you a thing or two about me. About my pa. He was just like you, acting all holier than thou. Just like you," I cried. "Got *that?*"

I waited for Tom to come back, to knock on the door and apologize. When he didn't, and I was left alone in the room, I pulled in my breath sharply, willing myself the one chance to find Pa and tell him how arrogant he had been to go traipsing across the Badlands. "What kind of ill-equipped man sets out on foot? On foot," I thought shuddering, "and crosses into an unknown?"

I yanked on the curtains and looked down onto a woman absentmindedly rocking her oversized baby buggy back and forth. It was covered with lace drippings, but I could still see a yellow-haired baby through the veil. The woman was talking to another bright-faced woman wearing a red fox collar who was eyeing this woman's mink just as suspiciously as I was eyeing the fox. I figured they were sweltering under all that pretense, but I didn't know. I had never worn fur before or been covered in lace. It seemed as though they were both ignoring the baby, but it didn't matter. Not to them.

As the women passed the hotel, I shouted to them as if by some chance they could hear me through the glass. "What choice do I have?" I called. "If I am going to demand an apology, or some kind of explanation as to why I was played with last night, then I will need the upper hand." I closed my eyes and cursed. "Equality, my ass. No woman is equal when she's in debt." I crammed a sweet roll into my mouth. "Edie, you're a fool," I told myself. "Get out, now. Go home. You can't win." I looked at the traveling frock and thought about the ramifications of stepping onto Mrs. Harrison's dance floor in goods that even she couldn't afford. She would take one look at me dolled up, lipsticked, and think her Charlie wasn't good enough for me. And then where would I be? Nowhere.

I reluctantly cracked open the top of a soft-boiled egg and slipped a silver spoon down into the pale yolk. It was all coming back now and I couldn't help but be pulled into the memory. I was twelve years old. Pa stood in the doorway of our meager apartment, a torn canvas rucksack in one hand and his tattered cap in the other. "I'm going, baby," he explained. I ignored him and rapped on the top of my soft-boiled egg with my knuckles to open it. I scooped out the partially cooked egg with a piece of broken shell. Bright yellow yolk ran down my fingers and into the palm of my hand as he explained this one. He oozed those words out of his mouth like hot taffy being poured onto a marble slab. "I'm goin', baby girl. Out West. Gonna find my due." I looked up at my pa with sorry eyes. "This time," he promised, "it's for real. Real gold."

"You're going to get yourself killed, Pa," I shuddered. "And then what will happen to me?"

He flinched. "It's foolproof, baby. And besides, we need the money."

"You'll just get yourself trapped knee-deep in quicksand..." At this, Pa laughed. "Strangled by boa constrictors. Trampled by woolly mammoths. Don't you get it, Pa?" I tried. "You aren't holier than thou," I complained, repeating the words I'd heard Ma use. "Can't you for once stop acting like you are?"

<>

I slipped my eager mouth over the dainty spoon and drank in the scent. My scent. I was soaked for real in geranium oil, my hair smoothed out, modern, and my delicate skin softened by the hot water, the creams, and the Madame's tonics. I looked around the spacious hotel apartment and thought about the likelihood of ever having one of my very own. My own porcelain clawfoot tub, my own window looking down on the fashionable street below, my own writing desk, my own library, my own telephone, I thought, tripping over my feet as I crossed the foreign terrain. I stumbled over the floor to the ladies' writing desk and picked up the heavy black telephone handle. I didn't know what to do with it so I studied it, and when there was nothing else to do, I tapped the black bar a few times, and waited.

A female voice, kindly and sweet, nothing like my mother's, answered. "Miss Ayres. How can we be of service?"

"Oh?" I said startled. "I am looking for...well, for...I don't know how you might find me...some salt?"

"One moment, please, and I'll connect you."

Another pleasant but gravely voice answered. "Room Service."

I questioned him. "Room Service?"

"Room Service, Miss Ayres. How can we be of service?"

"Room Service?" I sang astonished.

"We service the rooms, Miss Ayres, at the Waldorf-Astoria Hotel."

"Room Service," I trilled, "I need a dash of salt."

I closed my eyes and thought how unlikely it was that I was here when I should be there. When I opened them my eyes were on the silver coffee urn, the white cloth napkin, and the most unusually small silver spoon, but my mind was on Pa's rucksack. I picked up another one of the sweet breads and sank my teeth into it. Delicious ribbons of melted chocolate exploded into my mouth.

"Look up when I'm talkin' to you," came my father's slippery voice. I heard it as clearly as I had heard the deep voice on the telephone. I dropped the bread and looked around the room. It was eerie how real it felt. "Pass me the salt," I had said. "I'm leaving," he had said. "I don't believe you," I had said. And we went on like this until he dropped his rucksack on the rickety apartment floor and pulled an old wooden chair out from under the painted table. The chair was missing three of its four back spindles.

I pulled my eyes away from Mrs. Charles Harcourt's *The Blue Book of Etiquette*, put those eyes on him, and watched him sitting there, defeated. I peeled back the corners of his soul, that arrogant flagrant soul, with just one look. He turned away from me and tripped headlong into some cockamamy story about billiards, his due, about what was due, about who was due. And gold! My god, on and on about this forgotten safe deposit box filled with gold! My eyes went to my pa, to the yolk, and then to the eggshell spoon. In frustration, I threw my trembling hands heavenward toward Mother Mary. "You'll kill yourself, Pa, or get yourself killed. One or the other. Going to California."

He passed his cap from one hand to the other without much of a reason. "I have my Uncle Jimmy's money to collect," he explained. "I won't be gone long, and as soon as I collect my due I'll be home." He chuckled. "Quick as a bunny."

"No you won't. I know you. You'll fail at this too. And then what? You can't leave Ma and me alone to fail too." He shook his head and the tousled mat of black hair hung further down into his eyes. My voice rose. "You say you're coming home now, but how Pa? How? Not with all that swamp between here and California. All those alligators?" I stood and knocked the table out of the way. My egg toppled onto a stained mat. The yolk slid onto the faded pink and ran off the mat and down into the cracked table. By now I knew my way around a polished dance floor and had seen enough Greek tableaux to know where I stood in relationship to my pa. "You think you'll come back the hero with all this money. The hero of your own story. Is that right?" I shook the table. "It don't work out like that," I cried, slipping into my old voice. "The Argonauts died, Pa. People die. Ships at sea sink. Men perish."

"Baby girl," he cooed, stroking my trembling chin. "Your pa's not goin' across some per-i-lous sea. Or gonna be wrestlin' alli-gators." He smiled and took me into his arms. I could feel his heart beat strong against my cheek so I lay my head on that heart and soaked up all there was. "Your pa's no Argo-not." He chuckled. "No." He steadied his wide calloused hands on the table and then delicately, as if picking up individual grains of rice, scooped up every bit of spilled yolk from the cracks with a piece of burnt toast. "Here," he chimed, theatrically sprinkling a dash of salt over it. He bowed jauntily when handing the mess to me. "Eat this up, darlin' girl. And when it's your time you'll get your due. Mine's in 'em dug-up gold mines."

<>

I looked at my reflection in the hotel silver and poured myself a cup of hot coffee. I knew I should have stopped him. I could have, too. And that's what I will live with for the rest of my life. I put the silver spoon to my mouth and swallowed hard. It was a bitter memory, but there was no wet yolk to run down my childish hand. I tossed back the coffee. It went down smoothly. "No cracks in this sidewalk," I thought, skipping across the room and picking up the telephone receiver. Nothing like that at the Waldorf-Astoria. Was this my "God-has-plans-for-us" moment? My due?

I struck another Irene Castle pose. "Room Service please," I sang. I waited for the gravely voice to answer the phone, and when it did, I chirped. "This is Miss...um...Ayres in apartment...yes...the Heritage Suite." I laughed easily. "No, no photographs, but I could sign an autograph for you. I don't see why not. One more thing...if it's no bother. Some ice, please." I hung up the phone and immediately my mind went to my ma standing on the tips of her toes looking into that box of misplaced shoes in Woolworth's as if for all her life she'd been waiting to find her due. Her box of gold. I was beginning to see how it was now my box. I picked up the telephone again.

"Miss Ayres here," I chimed. "Thank you. You've been a doll. I need one favor. Just one," I began. "Could you send me that boy? The page. Yes, Mr. Ryan. Tom Ryan. That's the one. I do so need a hand moving my things." I smiled. It was easy to imagine the starlet's voice, her image, her words. I paused for effect. "My meager belongings." There were at least two dozen white orchids in the large crystal vase on the table, but I don't remember anyone coming into the room to replace the Casablanca lilies. I looked on the table for a card. Nothing.

"Connect me to the reception desk please," I continued. I pulled out one of the stems and waited. "Yes, this is she," I said easily. I paused. "Will I sign autographs in the Rose Room? This afternoon? Well, I don't know, Sir, if I can do that." I put the orchid to my lips. "No, I'm afraid that won't do. Studio rules you understand. I do have one favor to ask you though. Just one. Could we find a modest room for me? Yes. Modest, please. I don't need much. There's just too much to love about the Waldorf-Astoria. I think I'll stay awhile."

I hung up the phone. "These people are idiots," I thought laughing. I studied the dove grey traveling frock where it lay on the worn chintz. "I can't wear this. I just can't. He can't owe me one thing. Not one. And I most certainly don't want to owe him. Gad," I thought, feeling sick to my stomach. I burped up the sour taste of egg on toast and spun on my heels. "Get in here, Tom," I winced, scooping up Mr. Andino's expensive French goods and stuffing them back into the boxes. "You can work for me now."

VIII

I took the silk stockings out of their box to look at them again. I contemplated keeping them. I don't know why. When would I ever have the opportunity to own real silk again? Silk was something significant, I thought, retracing the steps in my mind back to Mr. Andino's room, his broad dark crimson curtained bed, and the hunger I must have felt when I lay, for the first time, upon eiderdown. Silk was not nothing. It said: I have arrived. I will belong. I am something. I am not nothing. Maybe Mr. Andino would never know that his kind, oh did I say kind, I meant manipulative, gesture had been refused. Would he even know that his gift had been returned to B. Altman? Maybe I could keep the stockings?

"Damn him," I winced. "I want these." I slipped my hands into each of the stockings and kissed them. "They fit me," I thought. "Don't they?" I wanted to try them on. I wanted. Something. But then I remembered the way Mr. Andino's hands had moved deftly up my legs, unsnapped the garters, and removed my hosiery from my legs with the finesse of some long-practiced dance step. "If I ever gave Mr. Andino the impression that I would sleep with him," I thought, "then I did so unintentionally."

I buckled. "I should have said *no* and really meant it. Didn't I? Oh, curse you and your cursing hand-me-downs, Edie. I deserve silk," I cried, holding the stockings to my lips. "Don't I? After all, I was the one who lost. Don't I deserve something too?"

I remember he cupped his smooth-as-silk hands on my bare skin as he caressed my shin, my ankle, my foot. "I really did win, didn't I?" he said purring.

"Won what, Sir?" I chirped.

He grinned. "Remember. No *Sir*. Just yes."

I pulled away. "No, Sir. Please."

"Stay awhile, Miss Ayres," he tried. "I just want to look at you."

"At me?"

"The belle of the ball. The will-o'-the-wisp." He grinned. "Will you dance for me?"

Eagerly, I leapt off the bed and danced, but that didn't stop him. Or me. I think the champagne stole my wits right out from under me. The more he poured, and the more he nestled those flatterings onto me, the more I drank up the taste of expensive uptown thoughts.

"You're something," he crowed.

"I'm me," I offered.

He laughed. "Do you come here often?" I shook my head. "But you want to? Am I right?"

"I don't know." I was telling him the truth.

"Lonely?" he continued.

I shot him a look of genuine surprise. "I don't know."

"I see it in your eyes. Not sad," he said, brushing a lock of hair off my forehead. "No. Lost." I turned from him and buried the hurt down into another taste of champagne. Another pirouette.

<>

"Maybe I don't need expensive things," I realized, looking at the orchids, the soft chocolate bread, and the Madame's thin porcelain china cup and saucer. "Or do I?" I gazed out the window to gauge the time, but everything was a blur of grey and imminent rain. I was hoping Ma would at some point use her wits and make the trek uptown to look for me, but only because I was beginning to think that I would need her. "How much time do I have?" I wondered, carefully sliding the delicate stocking onto my leg. "Not enough," I cursed. I pulled off the silk and thrust the stockings back into their box. Reluctantly, I stepped into last night's lemon chiffon and pushed at the buttons. "You can't accept them, Edie. Got that? If you do, he'll win."

There was a knock on the door and immediately it opened wide. A bellboy, dressed in a brown box jacket and matching brown pants, carried himself inside the room with an air of professional dignity. "We have your room ready, Miss Ayres," he said politely, if not a little nervously. He looked about the room for a moment and then stopped when he saw the unmade bed, the wet discarded towels on the floor, the cold breakfast tray, and the upturned pile of haphazardly stacked B. Altman boxes.

I followed his gaze and apologized. "You will forgive me," I offered. "It's been a hectic morning."

"Yes, Miss Ayres," he said swiftly. "Shall we?" he continued, gesturing to the door with a nimble, white-gloved hand. He looked down, through a pair of thick tortoise-shell frames, at my bare feet. He let his narrow eyes trace my figure. It was subtle and almost unnoticeable until he let his eyes linger on last night's lemon chiffon. "You don't have to explain," he offered. "We have guests who lose their luggage all the time. It happens. Porters at the station who can't be trusted, pilferers, souvenir hunters. Clowns, really," he said gesturing, stiffly, toward the boxes. "Shall we take these with us upstairs?" he asked. "I see someone has already come to your rescue."

"Oh these," I chimed, dismissing the boxes. "Too big. All of it. Sadly, it must be returned."

He nodded. "Pity. Would you like a car to take you down to B. Altman so that it can all be exchanged for a more appropriate size?"

"Exchanged?" I stammered. My head screamed *no*. Exchanging Mr. Andino's goods for new goods would still be the same as accepting his gift. "Oh no," I explained. "Tom will take care of this mess for me."

"Tom has been released," he said flatly.

I stopped dead in my tracks. "What do you mean?" I faltered. "You mean...sacked?"

"Yes, Miss Ayres."

"But..."

With a salute he touched his brown box cap and bowed. "We're terribly sorry for his rudeness."

"Rudeness?" I chirped.

"Please accept my apologies on behalf of the Waldorf-Astoria. You will not be charged for your room, Miss Ayres. None of the expenses." He scoffed ever so slightly, or so it appeared, and continued. "I have been told to take you to your suite where Mr. Boomer, the hotel manager, will greet you, personally."

"The hotel manager?" I croaked. "I don't understand."

"Tom was seen and heard," he stressed, "slamming this door, Miss Ayres. There were witnesses. 'We don't find fault often, but when we do we act upon it.'" He was reciting someone else's line, I could tell.

I nodded, but I could feel myself tipping and I reached out to grab ahold of his arm. "Such rudeness," I managed. "Indeed."

<>

I braced myself for the elevator ride to the third floor. I was sick to my stomach at the thought that Tom had been sacked, and all because of me. I tried to put on a smiling face, but the whole of the game was becoming too real and I didn't know how I was going to get off the court. My racquet strings were breaking one by one.

"Can I ask you a favor?" I tried, while stepping inside the steel cage. "Just one. Are you," I continued, stepping aside to make room for the bellboy to enter, "...do you have any way to reach him? This Tom." The young man took a step backwards, in a way that was rehearsed, as the elevator cage closed.

"We take the stairs, Miss Ayres," he explained, looking at me behind the steel trap.

I looked anxiously at the elevator attendant who, once again, did not meet my gaze. She stared at the floor, presumedly at my bare feet. "I haven't done anything wrong," I told her as we rattled up one flight, the elevator coughing as if the whole machine with her halting gears was struggling to breathe.

When the elevator came to an abrupt stop, the attendant pulled on the door. I stepped out of the box and put out my hands as if to reach for the sides of the crib. I held myself there for a minute until the bellboy came to greet me.

"This way, Miss Ayres," he said. "Follow me."

"My ma," I said uneasily, "will be looking for me."

Ignoring me, he continued, "This way."

"I know she'll be worried."

"We'll take care of you," he offered. "Nothing to worry about."

He turned the brass key in the lock and opened the door to an elaborately decorated room. This one was less opulent than the Madame's, but generously proportioned and alarmingly pink. I took a step back. Everything was covered in the same shade of salmon.

"Don't they have another can of paint around this place?" I complained.

"How would you like your drapes, Miss Ayres?" he asked, stepping into the room with the professional gait of a man. He was unlike Tom in every way. "Drawn? Or should they remain open?"

I looked at the fraying salmon pink silk drapery and braced myself. "Open. Thank you."

"Will that be all?" he asked, bowing slightly as he began backing his thin body out of the room.

"No," I said, pouncing quickly. "I'm in a terrible bind..."

He studied me from behind the thick lenses. "Perhaps Mr. Boomer," he said with a tone in his voice I didn't understand, "will serve you."

I coughed. "The hotel manager?"

"Never mind," he offered, gesturing toward a silver bucket of ice and a crystal glass sitting on one of the mahogany tables. "You're being well attended to. That's what we do here. But don't ask me for your personal favors." He held out a hand, expectantly.

I looked at the melting ice and then back at him, but his up-turned eyes were expressionless. He avoided eye contact. "What are you doing?" I asked. He looked down at his empty hand and then quickly placed it behind his back. "Do you have something against me?" I asked. "Personally, I mean?"

He turned the question back on me. "What do you have against us?"

"Us?" I asked. "Who? You?"

"You're playing us, Miss Ayres."

I stumbled. "Playing?"

"You come in here thinking we don't know you, but we know you. You're playacting the part of some..."

I was caught off-guard. "Some birthday girl?"

"No, but you're playing. I've watched you," he explained. "I saw you in the Astoria foyer this morning turning on the charm for..."

I winced. "For Tom?" The bellboy bowed and backed away. "Please," I said uneasily. "Don't bow to me. Please. I dislike it. I wasn't putting on the charm. I was..." He backed out of the room and out the door. "Please," I begged, following him out into the wide hallway. It was dark in the hall and not at all like my over-lit room. I preferred the shadow. I stepped uneasily across the patterned carpet and stood next to him. "I like you," I offered. "I don't know you, but I see you."

He shuffled away from me first with one step and then another. I hopped over the thorns and landed on one of the white asters. "You see, I can tell that you and I are very much alike." He looked down at me and frowned. "I mean it. We're not like most people. We put on airs, maybe, to get what we want, but who doesn't? You're putting on airs right now pretending you're not intimidated by me...a...um...starlet." He relaxed somewhat. "Don't you see how..." I said, searching for the best word, "how silly we both are?" I looked down at the thorns. "I'm trying to find a frock for a breakfast with Mr. Andino." He shot me a look of nervous, or was it suspicious, anticipation. "The Railroad Tycoon," I explained.

"Hotelier," he said, correcting me.

"Hotelier?" I shrieked. "I thought he was..." The young man bowed. This time his bow was genuine, less stiff, but I cringed. "Are you in the habit of doing that? That bowing? For me?"

He looked over the top of my head and into the salmon-colored room. "No, Miss Ayres, this is common."

"Common," I squealed, "to bow like I was..."

"A person of importance."

"But..."

He turned on his heels. I followed him down the hall and tapped him, frantically, on the shoulder. I bowed. "You're a person of importance. Aren't you?" I was genuinely confused about the bowing. I'd seen it all over the place last night. The nodding, the genuflecting, and now the bowing. He shot me another one of his suspicious looks. I laughed nervously. "Stop playacting with me," I explained. "You and I," I tried. "We're...we're..."

"We're what, Miss Ayres?" he said pausing. I detected something in his voice not unlike what I was feeling in that moment. He waited for me to answer, but all I could do was look up into his stubborn rehearsed grin. "You presume to know me?"

"We're not who we want to be. Here," I offered, pointing to the long hallway. "In our life. Now."

The young man stood stock-still and gazed down the empty hall. He turned his back to me and took a step, but then turned, unexpectedly, and looked me in the eye. This time I felt his steady gaze bore into me. "You're the most celebrated Hollywood starlet on the planet. The only one worth spending a hard-earned nickel for," he offered. I looked down at my feet, pained. "I saw *The Sheik* six times. And that, Miss Ayres, seems to me like a life worth living."

Embarrassed, I exclaimed, "I'm not her, you know. An heiress. I'm me."

"No, I know that, but you're..." He looked down the hall again and then turned to look behind him. "I can't get caught fraternizing or I'll get sacked."

"Oh my," I said surprised. "Of course."

He lifted his heels and stood on the balls of his narrow feet, eager to go. Or to stay. I don't think he could made up his mind. "I saw you dancing last night," he managed.

"Last night?"

"I stayed," he admitted, "to see if I could catch a glimpse of you this morning."

"You stayed because of me?" He nodded. "But you didn't know if you would see me?"

"No," he realized. He stood taller than my father, taller than Mr. Andino, and taller than Tom. Looking down at me he puffed up his chest. "You make life worth living," he swooned. "I mean that."

"You live for some fleeting glimpse of a starlet from the motion pictures? What's the point of that?"

"Not just any starlet."

I cocked my head and looked at him. He was serious. "I need help," I begged.

He lowered his heels and took a step away from me. The wheels in his mind were turning. I watched him step forward and then step away again. "Goodbye, Miss Ayres," he said, bowing formally. "It's been a pleasure serving you. And I wish you..." He stumbled and looked at me, the wheels turning again, the nerves returning. "I will forever thank you for this."

I grabbed his arm and pulled him, wordlessly, back into the room. "Don't put on airs with me," I sang, closing the door. "I need your help." He stood awkwardly with his hands behind his back, about as far up against the door as he could possibly stand. "Now look at me," I pleaded. "You and I both know how the game is played." He shot me a look of surprised interest. "Got that? I have to have this breakfast with Mr. Andino, the Hotelier," I said breezily. "He's expecting me. But I can't go downstairs in last night's frock," I explained, smoothing down the lemon chiffon. He froze. "And because the clothes that Mr. Andino sent to me were all...well, um...too big, I am going to need..."

He was seriously taken aback. His voice rose an octave. "I offered you a car, Miss Ayres. We can get any one of the hotel staff to escort you."

"I don't want an escort. I want you." He shot me a look of genuine surprise. "All this escorting here and there. It's irrelevant."

"I'll see what I can do," he managed.

"You're too kind," I said bowing. "Very kind. I can see it in your eyes. But that won't do. I need assurances." I turned from the bellboy and searched for the words I wanted to use. When they came out of my mouth they sounded pained, just as I had intended. "I was hurt," I began, "by Mr. Andino's offensiveness. I don't normally go with men," I tried. "Like that."

He interjected. "To their room."

I ignored him and went on. "I wasn't expecting things to go, well, to go the way they went. You see, I was only at the candy counter with Charlie when I heard the band and saw this trio of blondes trip down the hall. I wanted to follow them. They looked like they were off to someplace smart, dressed as they were. And I was, well, I had had my fill of chocolate malts." I stole a glance at the young man. "My fill of Charlie's insipid stories about the pony ring, you see." He stood before me as if questioning me. "No, you wouldn't see, would you?" I looked at him again, but he was waiting for me to continue. "I just wanted a taste of something fun. More fun than all that false pretense," I explained. "But Charlie wasn't interested in dancing. He said we didn't belong upstairs, for me not to go, but I wanted a look. One look. And Charlie..."

"Master Harrison," he said interrupting me. "Fine family."

I looked him over, pausing. "Fine family. Yes. We go way back."

"Your mother and his mother? His daddy and yours?" he offered as an explanation.

I nodded. "Something like that. And well, you see, I'm worried that Charlie will tell his mother who will tell..."

Relaxing, the bellboy laughed joyously. "This is the central dilemma in *The Malt Shop Fiasco*." I looked at him, struggling to understand. "*The Malt Shop Fiasco*," he repeated. "You know the one where that pretty teenage gal, oh what's her name, gets seduced by the handsome millionaire? I think he was a Steel Magnate. Something." The bellboy laughed again, easily, and pushed his glasses farther up onto his nose. "You're stealing the plot, Miss Ayres. Try another motion picture." He laughed again, this time harder.

"I beg your pardon?" I said. "I'm not stealing any plots. I'm trying to tell you my story."

The bellboy stepped through the door. "I won't get you a new frock. Not when Mr. Andino has generously offered you the best that B. Altman can provide. Take what you're offered, Miss Ayres, as a sign of affection." He laughed. "Obviously, your date to the confectionary didn't work out."

"No, no, it didn't, but you don't understand. I wasn't prepared to..."

He raised an eyebrow. "...to spend the night?"

"Insolent man," I complained, turning away from him. "Go. You're way too invested in my life. And you shouldn't be. It's crass."

IX

The bellboy tucked a piece of dirty blonde hair behind the box cap and adjusted the tight elastic strap. He pulled it away from his chin and then let it snap back in place. "It's simply a costume," I explained, pleading with him. He rose and fell, unwittingly, on his toes. "Just like you're required to wear." He frowned. "We're all playing a part. Motion picture or no motion picture," I tried. "And I need a new frock to, to..." I managed to find the word easily this time and I shouted, "to convince Mr. Andino I'm not in need. You see, he thinks I'm a starlet. You all do," I added. "I could never convince him otherwise." I waited for the bellboy to respond, and when he didn't, I stood on the tips of my toes. "I can't need him. Don't you understand? This isn't some motion picture. It's me."

"*The Sheik*," he sighed, taking in a breath and letting it out slowly as if finally understanding something puzzling. "Perhaps you're too independent, Miss Ayres. Too modern," he reasoned, looking at my bobbed hair, "for even the Waldorf-Astoria."

I shouted. "I'm me!"

"I'll see what I can do, Miss Ayres. I don't doubt you're in need," he said thinking, "but in favor of not appearing so."

"That's it!" I exclaimed.

"In need," he said, repeating this to himself, "but not wanting to appear so. Then you don't want rescuing?"

"I knew it!"

He smiled. "You don't want to be rescued by a millionaire tycoon because you don't want to appear..." He stopped and looked about the room. "Hungry."

I turned to look at what the bellboy was looking at. It was a dark round table, similar to the one in the Heritage Suite where Tom had placed the breakfast tray, but this one sat empty.

"Something like that," I realized.

"What motion picture is that from?" he asked, looking up and scrutinizing a water stain on the ceiling.

"I'm not starring in a motion picture," I explained. "I'm me."

"In need, but not so in need that you need rescuing." He nodded, pleased with himself.

"I need a new frock."

The bellboy pushed his hands onto his brown pants as if expecting to find a set of pockets. I guess when he realized what pants he was wearing, the hotel pair without a set of pockets, he turned on his heels as if to leave me quickly. "What about a pair of new shoes?"

I ran up to him and kissed him on the cheek. "Thank you. Oh, thank you," I squealed, wrapping my arms around his thin shoulders. "Please, tell me. What is your name?"

He smiled, showing off his clean white teeth. "Tom."

"No?!" I exclaimed. "Really?"

He nodded. "Here they call me Thomas, but Mother prefers Tom."

"You're a Tom?" I questioned. "I don't believe it. You're so unlike Tom."

He nodded. "Thomas it is then, Miss Ayres."

"I'm going to wait for you to bring me a new frock, Thomas. Something chic, but not too chic," I added.

He was finally pleased with me. I could tell. "You're not who I thought you would be." I looked up, surprised. Our eyes met. "You're fun," he admitted. "That I would have expected. You're daring, as all starlets probably are, but there's something different about you."

I didn't bat my eyelashes or do anything unnecessary now. I was getting undressed in a different kind of way and I wasn't sure I liked it. "Me?"

"What makes you so sure of yourself?" he asked. I shrugged. "No, Miss Ayres, it's a serious question. You weren't invited to that wedding banquet, were you?" He had me there and I shook my head. "And you just waltzed in there like you knew you'd be welcomed. That takes a certain kind of..."

"Stupidity," I realized.

He threw his hands to his heart. "No!" he countered. "My god you're something. I know you know it. Hollywood has its sights on you and I can see why. I see you," he offered. "That kind of confidence only comes when..." I relaxed somewhat and let him continue. I folded my arms across my chest and picked at one of the pink ribbons on my frock, all frill and outdated girlish charm. He thought about his words carefully, while giving me a look of genuine interest. "You know I think it comes about because you've been saddled with hurt. Haven't you? I see it in your eyes. But you're older now and coming to own that hurt."

I looked down at my bare feet and pushed at an imaginary castle door blocked by a hundred years of overgrown thorns. "Doesn't that still make me the damsel in distress? Now that I need you?"

"Aren't all girls in some sort of distress, Miss Ayres?" he offered.

"No," I shrieked. "My god, no." I was angry. "You're the one so sure of yourself, but now I'm not so sure of you."

"Relax," he said, impulsively taking ahold of my hand. "I'm going to charge it all to Paramount. Let them fix you up, Miss Ayres. It's on them to make sure you look the part every time you step out that door," he said, pointing to it. "That's not on me. I'm just the errand boy."

Thomas turned on his heels. He closed the heavy door, and the sound it made, so final, startled me. It was the same sound I had heard in our apartment all those years ago. I looked at the center table as if expecting a breakfast tray to be there, but the table sat empty. The entire room felt empty, devoid of anything charming or personal. I stared at the salmon moiré papered walls, the salmon bedside tables, the salmon drapes and then I turned toward the door expectantly. The room was hot. I marched across the floor and closed the drapes thinking it might help me feel better, but the silence only deepened. I continued to wait. I tugged on the lemon chiffon. I wanted it off. I wanted to forget everything about last night, so I ran my hands through my bobbed hair waiting for that joyous feeling of cutting it all off to return.

"Where are you, Thomas?" I thought, urging him to run my errand faster. "Please come back soon."

I toddled, uncharacteristically slow and lazy like, over the pink roses, the blue asters, and the red lilies. Lifting a pair of silver tongs, and fumbling brilliantly with them, I added another piece of slippery ice to the glass. I danced around the edge of the carpets and leapt from one sinking boat to another. I waltzed into the white-tiled bathroom, this one more cracked and aged than the Madame's, and stared at myself in the hotel mirror. I thought just how shocked Ma will be when she sees my hair. "Your curls," she will shriek. "Oh, my baby girl! Wha'd you go and do that for?"

"I'm sunk," I thought, putting my hands on the edge of the white pedestal sink and peering at myself. "Mrs. Harrison will disavow me this time for sure."

I stood back from the mirror. There was nothing right about last night's lemon chiffon. It now had all the tart and none of the sweet. I tore at the covered buttons. At Mrs. Harrison's insistence, I had agreed to wear it, this lemon meringue, but not before I had cajoled and begged her for something more grown-up. I told her there were more appropriate party frocks for girls my age, and when I showed her a picture of Irene Castle in her low-cut silver gown she threw her hands to her hips and chastised me. "I'll have no such flamboyance," she complained. "Nothing crass. You're too young, Edie. Stay young for as long as you can for if you don't the wolves will come to the door for you." I stared at her, uncertain. There wasn't a wolf I hadn't met, I realized, thinking about the greengrocers, the navy yard boys, the salt seller, and the bootblack sitting outside Mrs. Harrison's dance studio. Her telling me about the wolves was long past due.

What she was really telling me was that girls my age shouldn't look the part. We should look, oh I don't know, helpless.

<>

"I want this off," I stammered. "Worthless girl. Worthless." In my haste to pull the frock down over my shoulders it ripped. All along the ruffled neckline the chiffon puckered and tore. I shrieked. "Oh Mrs. H., I didn't mean to do that. Truly."

This time I sat on the edge of the deep clawfoot tub and really cried. I didn't know just how powerful buried feelings like these could be. In my mind the heavy door closed, over and over, just as it had closed the day my pa left. In a single swift motion our lives changed from bad to worse, from trapped to clipped. Not even the war or the influenza had brought on this much need. I touched my bobbed hair. The emptiness of that day had returned and I stared at the bathroom door willing it, too, to slam shut. "You're not coming back, are you, Pa?" I cried. "Tell me once and for all. You're nowhere now, aren't you?" I cried harder. "You've gotten yourself nowhere." I tore at the frock and it ripped all down the side. When I stepped out of it I kicked the frock, frantically, under the tub.

I couldn't stop the tears. They came on now with force. "Don't leave me, Thomas," I stammered, wiping my runny nose on the back of my hand. I was crying for Ma, for me, and for certain I was crying for Pa. "Idiot girl," I wailed. "I should have begged Pa to stay." I pulled on the cold handle and ran water into my sweating palms. I splashed my face and stood in front of the mirror willing the tears to stop. "Don't leave me to rot,

Thomas," I thought, suffocating in the overheated room. Standing in my perspiration-stained slip, I could hear the sounds of Fifth Avenue. There was a clattering of wheels on the pavement and I could tell immediately that it was a cart being pushed along the street. "Pa," I cried, running to the window, "is that you?" I threw back the drapes. "Where are you?" I shouted.

I peered out the window and watched a young girl in a pair of large wooden clogs struggle to push a heavy flower cart down the street. Her younger sister toddled beside her in a matching dirty muslin frock and was equally unkept, except for the tidy blonde braids. They turned from me and together they continued pushing their broken cart down the street. "I know where you are, Pa," I cursed, yanking the drapery closed. "You're nowhere. But I'm somewhere," I realized, looking about the hotel room. "Got that, Pa? I'm finally somewhere."

I threw my arms around my body and held myself in an awkward embrace. I took a deep breath and sat down on the edge of the bed to wait. I was hesitant to lie down and ruin the waves so I tucked my feet under me and counted: 1-2-3. 1-2-3. 1-2-3. In my mind I was waltzing with Mrs. Harrison, with Charlie, with my pa. But sometime last night I had been left alone with Mr. Andino. "Idiot," I cursed. "I should have said *no* when he clambered up the grand stairs after me insisting I must be Agnes Ayres."

I was tipping sideways thinking about last night. I remembered the ballroom doors ready and waiting to be opened for me when I returned from my waltz down Peacock Alley, when Mr. Andino came galloping up behind me, when he took my hands in his, and laced his hungry fingers through them. I felt a jolt of uncertainty, but I let him slip Mrs. Harrison's long white gloves back on. He traced his hands deftly over mine, but he had to tug at the gloves to get them to go on over my perspiring palms. He did this with great effort, but was loath to let me, or anyone else, notice. "Miss Ayres," he pounced, "you do me the honor."

The doorman, unaccustomed to smiling, managed a grin as he pulled on the doors. They flung open to the rambunctious din of overdressed men and women in need of another dance, in need of cheer, in need of petting as they jostled one another clamoring to get the best look, the best seat, the better view. I was instantly assaulted by flashbulbs and I threw my hands to my eyes. There was a hand on my arm and a camera in my face. "Miss Ayres," they shouted. "Come with us....Polish our seat....No, ours....Over here, Miss Ayres," came yet another chorus of turbulent voices.

"Do pardon," cautioned Mr. Andino, bracing himself, and then me with a protective arm around my waist. "Miss Ayres will be with you momentarily."

If I swooned I did so unintentionally. In front of the un-abashed revelry, the bass drums, the trombones, the saxophones, the pulsating dance floor, the feathers, the beads, the clatter, and the flash and smoke of camera bulbs, Mr. Andino whisked me from the open ballroom door and carried me upstairs to his room. It all happened so quickly I didn't know how I had arrived, but only that I had been taken to a bed, his bed, a bed so plush and inviting I couldn't help but lie down.

<>

"Oh my god," I howled, throwing my hands into the air. "There are photographs of me in all the papers. That's what Tom was trying to tell me!" I nearly choked on the thought: *The New York Times.*

I curled into a fetal position on the splintered floor and rocked myself back and forth until I was calm. It had been far too long since Thomas had left me alone. He should have returned by now. I was convinced someone had seen my photograph in the Sunday paper, figured out the game, and turned me in. Now he would come upstairs and drag me out of here. It was only a matter of time. I counted the minutes. The minutes dragged until I was certain another hour had passed. I stood up and peered at the ice. Melted. I opened the drapes. The street was active, not busy, but active. A steady stream of people dressed in their Sunday best paraded up and down the muddy sidewalk, hesitantly, as they dodged the spray from the motorcars hitting last night's rain-soaked potholes. "There are cracks in the sidewalk, Ma," I realized. "Even here on Fifth Avenue."

X

I leaned over the bathroom sink and drank greedily from the faucet. I was so thirsty, my head pounding, that I felt like a mangy camel miraculously finding an oasis after weeks in the desert. Not a soul had come to check on me. My stomach was in knots and I thought, "What is keeping Thomas?" I splashed cold water on my face and looked at the droplets as they fell, like tears, down my cheeks. "Just how bad off will Tom and his sister be now that he's been sacked?" I asked the mirror. I looked at the reflection before me, that of a stupid girl, or maybe that of a starlet, I didn't really know anymore, and wiped the tears. "Maybe the starlet can help Tom get his job back," I realized, "but I still have no idea who Mr. Andino really is. And why isn't he asking for me?" Immediately, I scratched that thought. Mr. Andino had no business coming to my aid. For all that I think he did to me, I had no business asking for him. I was wronged.

The angry tears came on strong now. These were not the "I'm feeling sorry for myself" tears. I studied my snarled-up face in the mirror. "I was wronged," I hissed. "Do you hear that, Pa?" I continued, pointing a shaking finger at the mirror and cursing. "I was wronged." I leaned on the edge of the sink and replayed the scene. Over and over this day got replayed: the tableaux, the spilled egg, the burnt toast. His chafed hand on mine one last time.

"You're not really going to leave us, are you, Pa?" I shuddered, slamming *The Blue Book of Etiquette* down onto the table. "Why now? Why when we're doing so well?" He sopped up the runny egg with a piece of burnt toast and handed me the mess. "We don't need an inheritance. Why would we? I have Mrs. Harrison on my side now, Pa. You've got your taffy cart. We're both peddling like real hoofers now, Pa. You can't leave us," I cried. "We're hoofing it," I trilled, demonstrating a series of intricate tap-dancing steps. "We're going places, Pa. Look at us. That's all we need. A couple of dancing lessons. You and me." Awestruck, Ma struggled to keep her tongue as she watched me dance around the kitchen table. "We're going places. Aren't we?" I cried, picking up Mrs. Charles Harcourt's rules for living and shoving it in his face. "'When the mind has been trained to habitual right thinking, the result is instinctive right action,'" I wailed. "Isn't this true, Pa? You and me. Together. Isn't that right action?"

<>

I slipped my hands off of the porcelain sink and smoothed my hair. "I don't know how we've managed, Pa, for this long," I thought, turning off the cold handle and pulling on the hot. "How we've managed without you." I looked at myself in the mirror. "How?" I winced, touching my trembling hands to my face. The Madame's creams and tonics were beginning to itch so I scrubbed my face frantically with a bar of Ivory soap. I sat down on the edge of the tub, defeated, and inhaled deeply. "I have no business being here," I realized. "None."

I pushed my way over the bedroom floor, and instead of leaping over the thorns, I stumbled through them. I picked up the heavy black telephone receiver and waited.

"Good afternoon, Miss Ayres," came the pleasant voice on the other end.

I coughed. "There's been a mistake. I shouldn't be here."

She sang, "Oh no, Miss Ayres, there's no mistake. We're sending you Mr. Boomer, the hotel manager," she explained, "straight away. He's been detained."

"Detained?"

"On behalf of the Waldorf-Astoria. Please. The press. He's doing his best to contain them all."

"The who?" I asked, falling down into the salmon-colored boudoir chair.

"Straight away," she promised. "Connecting you, Miss Ayres."

"I'm trying to tell you that I'm not her," I insisted. I listened for a response. "Hello?" Again, I paused. "Hello?"

The deep familiar voice on the other end of the telephone line boomed, "Room Service, Miss Ayres. We have your luncheon on the way."

"You do?" I asked. "Who…"

"Kindly be patient," he suggested. And he hung up the phone.

I ran my hands down my wrinkled cotton slip. "Room Service. Why didn't I think of that?" There was a sudden knock on the door. "Thomas?" I squealed. "Come in!"

A page, wearing Tom's ill-fitting navy blue suit with all its brass buttons now attached, opened the door, took one look at me half-dressed, and struck a pose. He bowed lifting only his arms to me as if presenting a queen with her scepter and barked, "Your linens, Miss Ayres."

"Linens?"

Without raising his eyes to me, he carefully placed a heavily starched pile of bed linens into my arms. "Your luncheon will be served shortly," he said abruptly, before taking a militant step backwards and closing the door behind him.

I opened the door and looked down the corridor, but the young page was eagerly making his way back down the dark hall. "He didn't even ask for an autograph," I thought, puzzled. Looking once more up and down the long hallway, hoping for a glimpse of Thomas, I closed the door hesitantly and tossed the impeccably clean white linens onto the bed. They were stitched in white thread with a large geometric <AA> pattern on the hem. I studied the stitching, at first questioning it, but when I realized that someone had made them up for Agnes Ayres personally, I laughed. I actually laughed out loud.

I had no way of knowing then how valuable the bed linens would become, never having placed any kind of value on wrinkled old bedsheets before. But in time, and I will tell you just how this came to be, the bed linens would be auctioned off, as would everything in this room, to the highest bidder who paid to take a piece of me home.

The room was silent. It was a heavy, empty silence unlike anything I was accustomed to. Our apartment was deafening, I realized, thinking how onerous it would be to return to the constant squeal of filthy children in the gutters, the anxious calls from across littered alleyways, the arrogant responses, the barking dogs, the clattering trains, and the constant yapping of my ma with her irritating nasal inflections. I didn't need to return to the broken carts, the sagging telephone wires, and the smell of urine in the street.

I stood on the tips of my toes and let the words drip from my tongue like melting butter. "Kindly, be patient. You will be served shortly. On behalf of the Waldorf-Astoria," I rehearsed. The words tumbled easily. "Room Service please," I laughed, hopping onto the bed. Thrilled at the prospect that I hadn't been discovered, I pulled Agnes Ayres' bed linen over my body and drank in the scent. It was maybe gentle like lavender laundry soap, but real like bleach. It took a long time to identify what the linen smelled like. "Like new," I thought smiling.

I rolled over and stared at the memory of a tall, wiry man with a wax mustache, who, as I was remembering it, had been sleeping next to me this morning. Lying naked next to a man was not something I had ever thought about. My lens is wide. It is not narrow like the lens most girls my age have who think only of marriage. I think about dancing. I think about putting my left foot in front of my right and seeing where the steps will lead. I don't think about falling in step behind someone else. I've seen the hurt my pa has caused and I don't want that kind of marriage. I don't want to wake up and have to fry my own egg on a skillet battered by years of neglect.

Startled, I sat up and looked around the room. "How did I even get here, Pa? Me? Edie May? I should have stayed home where I belong."

I looked at the empty space beside me on the bed and thought about how easily I had slipped out of Mr. Andino's bed this morning, and in the still-dark room, pulled the cool linen sheet back over his naked shoulder. I remembered looking down on him, questioning what I should do. I was desperate to go to the bathroom, desperate to rinse my teeth, desperate to put the lemon chiffon back on and tiptoe out of the room, but there were too many closed doors in his apartment. I didn't know which door led where. Mr. Andino stirred and I slipped back into the bed. I lay as still as I could until the urge to go began to burn. I shot out of bed and ran across the darkened room. "Please, Mother Mary," I prayed, opening a polished door, "let this be the right one."

<>

I closed my eyes willing it all to go away, like the end of a melodrama tableaux, but the memory of what I had seen and done was hard to erase. I had spent the night with a man who stole my virginity. "And I let him, Mother," I whispered, pulling the crisply laundered sheet up over my head. "I didn't mean to. It just happened."

XI

I settled down on the bed and waited. I counted 1-2-3. 1-2-3. 1-2-3. Mrs. Harrison's triumphant booming voice was in my head. "Take it to the room, Edie. That's my girl. Give me that gorgeous smile. That's the one. Look up, Edie. Always, my pet, look up."

There has to be more to this life than a series of memorized dance steps, the reluctant turn of a cheek, or a set of hungry peepers looking down at me. I closed my eyes, struggling to remember just who I was, or who I should be. I must have danced prettily for Mr. Andino. Didn't he ask me to? I remembered sashaying over the thorns in his room as if Mrs. Harrison were watching me perform. I remembered Mr. Andino pouring more of his illicit champagne into a crystal glass for me, and as the steps got freer, magically, I think I began to tip more wine about the room without a care in the world. I drank in that feeling of dancing without Mrs. Harrison's steely eyes on me, without her sharp tongue, and without that rod. My god, the rod. "Point your toes, Edie," she would say while pointing a long wooden rod, an extension of her gnarled finger, to the floor. "Unfurl your fingers, Edie. Dance pretty, Edie. Dance as if the world were watching you."

I looked down onto the street below. "The world is watching me now, Mrs. H.," I shuddered, thinking about the Sunday *New York Times*. I picked up the telephone receiver and waited. When the unknown voice on the other end answered, I held my breath. "Yes, this is she. Thank you. Yes, I would be happy to. If you could please send Thomas," I decided, "I will sign it for you. Yes, Thomas, the bellboy." I frowned. Had I heard her correctly? "Gone home?" I shrieked. "Without me?"

I threw the receiver down and cursed. "Son of a bitch. Goddamnsonofaflimflamman." My hands shook, but I pulled frantically on the telephone cord that dangled over the edge of the table. "Hello?" I wailed into the mouthpiece. "Are you there?" Nothing. She was gone. I dropped the earpiece into the cradle where it landed with a heartbreaking thud. "Thomas, how could you? Not you too," I cried. I sat down on the edge of the bed knowing that I had finally come to the end of the show. I ran my hands over the tears and cursed Thomas. "You idiot," I winced. "You and I...we could have gone places."

There was a sharp knock on the door and I sprang from the bed. "Thomas?" I chimed.

Through the hotel door I heard that deep familiar voice croon, "Your luncheon, Miss Ayres."

I ran my perspiring hands down my cheeks, and with aplomb, like a starlet, at least like the ones I've seen on the motion picture screen, I opened the door. A delicate man with dark willowy hands nodded to me, then lowered his head as he pushed an overladen table into the room. I watched the table, covered in a white linen cloth that fell to the floor, float, as if on air, over the carpets. I leapt over the thorns and landed on a white aster. "Thank you kindly," I sang. "How hungry I am." The dignified waiter, dressed in a black jacket and trousers and long white starched apron, looked up at me and grinned. His dark eyes, soft and warm, like pools of ancient knowledge, met mine. If he noticed that I was half-dressed it didn't appear to disturb him.

"I come to you, the pauper," I said, extending my trembling hands. The words came out spontaneously. They were unrehearsed.

He lifted his head of wiry white hair slightly and grinned. In that hotel voice I had come to know from the other end of the telephone, he bellowed, "'Tis my pleasure to serve you, Miss Ayres." With fanfare, he placed a chair next to the little table and motioned, with a wave of his impeccably clean gloved hand, for me to sit. I did so. He pushed in the chair. Then he discreetly slipped a piece of hotel stationery across the table indicating that I should sign it, which I did, with the name AGNES AYRES in a large childish scrolling hand. He beamed, retreated backwards, and closed the heavy door behind him.

I stared at the table. It was covered in several silver domes that looked like dented manhole covers. I tapped a silver spoon onto one of them. It rang like the gong on Mrs. Harrison's dance floor. "Is it time to switch partners?" I thought, lifting the lid. I winced. "Son of a bitch."

It had become all too easy to curse, all too easy to put myself back into a pair of ill-fitting shoes, and all too easy to remember Pa's leaving. I pulled once more at the memory of the burnt toast, the spilled egg, and the splinters my father got in his rough knuckles as he swiped them over the old wooden table to retrieve the yolk. "Son of a goddamn bitch," he yelled. I took his injured hands in mine, but he pulled away abruptly. "I'm asking for one favor, baby. Just one," he choked, sucking on his hands where the splinters had lodged into his chafed skin. "One favor. You're a big girl now..."

"Then why are you calling me a baby?" I thought.

"...and big girls don't cry. Big girls..." he explained, but the words got stuck in his throat. He scooped me up in his arms. "Please, Edie. Don't hurt." I put my wet cheek on his fraying coveralls and breathed in the scent of warm taffy. "Let me take the hurt for you, Edie." I lifted my chin and looked into his ruddy face. It was so full of hope. "I'll be back before you know it. Your pa's not goin' across some per-i-lous sea. I won't be wrestlin' alligators." I clung to him, but he pried me off his chest and pulled away. "I'm not some Argo-not. I'm me. And I'm askin' you for one favor, Edie," he beamed, offering the sopped-up egg toast to me, and bowing before retreating out the door. "One favor. Be strong."

Ma was wringing out Pa's shirts in the sink and standing silently in the steamed-up room. She covered her eyes with the back of one hand and swatted at something with the other. A fly? A roach? It was the first and only time I remember her not saying a thing. I looked at her as if to urge her to do something, stop him, curse, cry, but she threw her hands into the air and spun on her heels.

<>

My pa is gone. Lost somewhere on his way. Lost. My pa has lost his way. I pulled at the tear in my heart and reached for a tall glass of bright red juice. It was sharply flavored, but I drank it down without really stopping to enjoy it. I was ravenous. I sucked on the celery stick, reached for the silver pitcher, poured myself another glass, then tossed the heavy silver manhole cover onto the bed. "Eggs again," I cursed. "Son of a bitch."

The telephone rang and I nearly leapt out of my skin. I had never before heard a phone ring, I realized. Never. The chair fell to the floor as I shot out of it. I took a deep breath, steadied myself, and as practiced as I could be, I picked up the receiver.

"Miss Agnes Ayres," I sang, testing my voice.

His voice was high and shallow. "This is Mr. Alfred Banks, Miss Ayres. Concierge."

I hesitated. "Yes?"

"We have a delivery for you."

"For me?"

"Shall I have it sent upstairs?"

I was genuinely surprised. "For me?"

"From B. Altman."

"Oh, heavens," I whistled. "It's about time. Yes, please. Do send..." He hung up the phone. "Hello? Hello?" I tossed the earpiece down and sprang to my toes. I danced over the garden of wool roses. "Thomas, you did it!" I exclaimed, throwing open the door, and peering down the hall.

The anxious flutters in my stomach returned as I stood looking for him. "I knew you'd be smart about it, Thomas," I whistled. "You're perfect!" I took a running leap down the hall and hopped from one red lily to another. I turned around and ran back in the other direction, this time crossing one leg over the other, and twirling midair.

When I saw the staunch starched seamstress marching her wide hips down the hall toward me, I dropped to the floor. She looked at me curiously. "Miss Ayres," she remarked, with a nod of her head indicating that I should return to my room.

"It's about time," I winced. "Where's Thomas?"

"Who?"

"The bellboy?"

She said something unintelligible and crossed the room, again with that air of stiff confidence. She looked at the plate of cold poached eggs, picked up the fallen chair, and dropped a smaller stack of B. Altman boxes down onto one of the decorative round tables. Frowning crossly at the manhole cover lying upturned on the bed, she chirped, "Ya're unconcerned?"

I studied the eggs, willing them to go away, as she followed my gaze back to the luncheon tray. "I dislike eggs for luncheon," I tried.

She turned from me sharply, lifted the white tablecloth, and placed the domed silver service cover on a shelf under the table to hide it from view. "Eat yar luncheon, Miss Ayres. Ya're gonna need it." I took a step back from her and shook my head. "Eggs Benedict. With hollandaise. A Waldorf-Astoria Hotel spec-i-ality," she explained. She picked up another piece of hotel silver and poured out a thick yellow sauce. Then she bowed slightly, with a small nod of her head, and handed me *The New York Times*. "Are ya really unconcerned?" she asked, pointing to the "Social Notes." I snatched the paper from her and scanned the page anxiously, reading every word. "No mention of ya, Miss Ayres," she bellowed. "Not one word."

I turned the paper over. "Is that all there is?"

"Not one word. An' all 'em nosey reporters downstairs too," she added. "They weren't gonna let me attend to ya, but I insisted," she continued, reaching for the hem of my cotton slip and pulling it off over my head with one quick extracting motion.

"Is that what you're doing?" I asked. "Attending?" I crossed my arms over the brassiere. It had been my mother's, but it was too big and I was self-conscious that it gaped. "Where's Thomas?" I asked.

She unhooked my brassiere, folded it up, then changed her mind and discarded it onto the bed with a flick of her wrist. "We'll get ya ready for the cameras," she said, looking me over approvingly. "They're waitin' for ya in the foyer."

I scanned the newspaper one more time. "Mrs. Ogilvie will be closing her apartment tomorrow," I tried. "300 Park Avenue."

The seamstress puckered her lips. "She'll be travelin' to Bar Harbor for the summer." I lifted my eyes to hers. "It don't bother ya?" she complained. "That ya're not mentioned?"

"I imagine they respect my privacy," I said, with a flick of my own wrist to indicate the salmon-colored room.

This pleased her. She clapped her hands. "My god," she bellowed, "this place really is high class."

"It's the Waldorf-Astoria," I trilled. "Where you can have a bath in your own room." I looked at the hollandaise sauce pooling on top of the poached eggs on toast and laughed. "And Room Service."

We both laughed easily. She looked at me and sighed. "I'm so nervous," she admitted.

"Heavens," I squealed. "Whatever for?"

"Meetin' ya. Havin' this honor." She stood back and looked over my skinny bones. She let out another long sigh. "Ya're smaller than I would have imagined, but I think this time we have the smartest little frock for ya."

"Don't think you don't know me," I offered.

"I'm tryin'."

Our eyes met. I felt her studying me in a way that was good. She wasn't undressing me with her eyes the way Tom did, or looking to peel back my soul from my body the way I felt Thomas might have been doing. No, she was a godsend, this seamstress of mine, come to get me out of here. "I liked the...um...traveling frock," I said stuttering, "but it was difficult to accept. You see...I was...um...compromised. And it was too much. Too much to ask of Mr. Andino. Too expensive," I tried. "It put me in a compromising position to accept such a gift. I just couldn't." She nodded. "There's nothing I want more than to waltz up to him," I lied, "and offer him my immense gratitude." The words flowed effortlessly. If she curtsied she did it ever so slightly. "But alas," I tried, "the gesture was too grand. I'm really a simple woman at heart."

The seamstress sprang to her toes and pulled open the first of the boxes. "This design," she offered, "comes from..."

I think I swooned when I first put my eyes on the frock. "Please. Tell me..."

"Paris," she said smiling. I stood on the tips of my toes so that I could be taller next to her. She threw the silk frock up against my pale skin and hooted. "The cameras will love ya." The frock was cut on the bias, very avant-garde, explained the seamstress, and cut low to enhance my small breasts. The unadorned, and unapologetically simple, navy blue frock had but two thin straps that would slip over my shoulders, she explained. No buttons or bows. She swooned, "Nothing to take away from the beauty of the person wearing it."

The seamstress opened another box, and with the tenderest of touches pulled out the lace-trimmed underpinnings from the thin paper. We both swooned at the sight of the lavender silk. "It's stunning," I gasped. "What is it?"

She smiled proudly. "It's all ya need."

"No corset?" I asked, looking into the empty box.

"Ya don't need it. So why wear one?" I lay my hand on my slim tummy and smiled. "Here," she grinned, handing me the imported camisole. "Get dressed. There's no time to waste."

I stepped into the plunging lavender silk one-piece and marveled at how easy it would be to get dressed in the morning. I'd be ready in a flash, I thought, now that they were making bloomers and a bandeau as an all-in-one. I turned to her. "No garters?"

"This is better," she explained. "Ya have such beautiful legs, Miss Ayres. Why not show 'em off?"

"No ill-fitting hosiery," I remarked, marveling at the thought.

"No strappin's," she explained.

With the same kind of fanfare I once saw at Mr. Ziegfeld's follies, one of those dance extravaganzas Mrs. Harrison insisted she take me to, the seamstress reached up over my head and slipped the navy blue dress over my shoulders. The elegant frock cascaded easily down over my slim hips and fell in a swirl just below my knees. "We had it made specially for ya."

I stuttered. "For me?"

"An' these," she sighed, reaching for another white box and extracting a long string of black pearls, "are a Parisian design from another one of 'em up-and-comin' designers. Chanel." She tied the pearls in a knot at the end of the strand where they swung, in an irreplaceable fashion, down to my waist. "Pearl earrings to match," she cheered, taking a pair of black pearl drops out of the box. "An' this," she sang, slipping a tidy matching blue shantung silk hat down over my bobbed hair to finish it off. "That's it. That's all ya need." She reached into the pocket of her grey smock and pulled out a slim gold tube of lipstick. "I kept this," she confessed. "For myself." The seamstress handed me the lipstick. "But it's really yars."

"No," I said, with a wave of my hand. "Keep it."

I sensed the regret in her voice. "I can't."

"But of course you can. Mr. Andino will never know."

"No, no, that's true," she said, "but his accountant will. An' if I don't hand it over to the rightful owner who can account for all of this," she said, sweeping her hands over me like I was now property to be accounted for, "then..."

"Are you telling me," I said faltering, "that Mr. Andino knows..."

She ran her steady hands down my new Parisian-inspired frock to smooth it out, then stood back to admire me. She put her hands on her wide hips and took a stance. "He's the Architect."

I threw my hands into the air. "Now he's an Architect?!" I exclaimed.

"Oh, I don't know what he is, but isn't he grand?" she said, eyeing me proudly.

Defeated, I sat down on the bed and took off the hat. "No. He's evil."

"He's tryin', Miss Ayres, an' this time I think we plumb nailed it."

I took her calloused hands in mine and pulled her down next to me. "Damn him," I confessed. "Damn him and his charm. His money. This," I wailed, sweeping my hands over the ghastly room. "What am I doing here? Truly? Why have I been so reluctant to leave?"

The seamstress shot up off the rickety old wooden bed, looked at me to apologize for sitting, crossed the room, and then, with effort, turned to face me. She stood for a long time, in a pair of battered black brogues, surveying me. I looked down at her feet and she blushed. Finally, she spoke. "Ya will make the studio proud."

I stood up and swayed, first to the left foot and then to the right. I took a step and walked over to her. "What about me? How will I be proud? Ever?"

"Ya don't have to be proud, Miss Ayres, ya're..."

"I'm nobody," I cringed. "Got that?" She drew in a sharp breath. "Can't you understand? Aren't you a nobody too?"

XII

The seamstress stood with her hands clasped behind her wide bottom and exhaled. "I'm not a nobody." If she was hurt by my remark, she didn't say. She stood taller and looked about the room. "I'm on my way to becomin' senior stitcher. At Altman's. An' my name is Beatrice Walsh." I looked up from the unfashionable shoes and into her broad ruddy face. She was not pained, nor did she seem overly concerned, but I could tell from the way she set her teeth that she was holding her tongue. "An' ya're not a nobody either," she offered. "We've made ya into somethin'." She stood back and surveyed me. "I'm a part of that." She stalled for a moment and then displayed a wide, toothy grin. "We need ya Miss Ayres. Ya're someone to look at. To..."

"And you're proud?" I asked, challenging her. "Proud to own..."

"Not own, Miss Ayres. Admire."

I gasped. "What is there to admire? I'm a stupid girl."

She smiled. "Come now. We all make mistakes." I narrowed my eyes. "An' ya're no saint," she said softening.

I was offended. "I'm not trying to be a saint."

She came to me, palms together, and bowed. She replaced the hat and tucked a piece of my hair back in place, making sure that one of the spit curls would be seen. "No. God doesn't want His saints to be starlets, now, does He?" Flabbergasted at the thought, I shook my head. "An' besides. Ya're a lass. A little down on yar luck at the moment, but that's because ya're not married." I waved my arms back and forth to say *no no no*. She grinned. "We've all been followin' ya in the magazines, Miss Ayres, admirin' ya from afar, ya know. All us girls in the work-room." She pointed down the street toward B. Altman. "We just love ya. An' we need this. This," she said, waving her hands admiringly over my new frock. "Ya're an Independent, but..."

"That's only a persona," I offered, "from a role in a motion picture. That's not me."

"True," she said thinking. "But as an Independent..." Again, she looked down at me and grinned. "...ya set the stage. Get married a second time if ya want. Or not..."

I squealed. "Again?"

She grinned. "Oh, come now. It's not that bad." She tipped her hips to me in a bawdy way. "I love my Danny Boy."

I was clear. "I don't need marriage. Not now. Not yet."

"Ya can't always be so unlucky, Miss Ayres. See if ya don't win a few more hearts along the way." She turned to leave. "Gracious, I almost forgot the pièce de résistance," she cried, over-pronouncing the words and clapping her hands. "That's French."

Disappointed, I turned from Beatrice and, once again, took off the hat. I tossed it into the chair. "I thought you were some-body different, but you're too exacting for me."

If she wanted to ignore me she wasn't doing a very good job. I watched her set her teeth again. "Your shoes," she said, recovering, crossing to the table, and curtsying as she handed me the box.

I studied her. "How come you're so happy?"

She smiled. "Meetin' ya, Miss Ayres. It's the thrill of a lifetime."

"And you think I'm…"

Beatrice looked at me and swooned. "Oh, ya're just a gem! One of 'em figures. One of 'em women everyone looks to, to gauge their own worth." She was satisfied with her answer and she nodded, pleased.

I sat down on the bed and reluctantly opened the box. I thought about what she had just said. "It's not that I don't want love, it's not that. Oh, I don't know, Beatrice, please tell me you don't think I will need to get married. Even if I should. My Pa made that one very clear."

"I didn't say ya should or ya shouldn't. I said ya have a choice." I took her at her word, but she was still thinking I was Agnes Ayres who was divorced, a true Independent.

I took the shoes from their box. They were wrapped in a piece of thin pink paper. I unwrapped them, and when I did my heart just about leapt out of my chest. In my hands I held a delicate pair of satin-heeled slippers that had been dyed to match the frock. I lifted them to the light. "By god," I cried, with tears of joy coming on. "These are spectacular." I looked into Beatrice's smiling eyes and grinned.

"Ya like them?"

I swooned. "I love them."

She bowed. "I was hopin' so."

I slipped the unadorned shoes onto my bare feet and buckled the thin straps. "You really do know me, don't you?"

Beatrice grinned. "I'm tryin'."

"Simple," I said, standing and admiring them. "And comfortable."

"The most elegant design comin' from the salons of Paris."

"Made-to-order? For me?"

She nodded. "Made for a star."

I stood a little taller and waltzed easily over the thorns, but when I looked down onto the busy street below, I stopped suddenly. "I owe somebody," I realized, looking at a battered taffy cart. "And it's against my better judgement to owe Mr. Andino for all this," I tried. I was so conflicted, and hurt, and frightened. And I knew it. I was trapped. It was becoming obvious I was never going to find Pa alive. And even if I did I wouldn't know him. I turned to Beatrice and winced. "What will happen to me now that I'm dressed in goods I don't deserve?"

Beatrice was gentle. "Take it all as a present, Miss Ayres."

"But don't you see?" I cried. "This is all...well, it's all so heavy. A burden."

"Yar frock is practically weightless," she reasoned, crossing the room with the hat in her hands.

"It's not the frock, Beatrice. It's me." There was no use trying to explain it to her. She would never understand. Beatrice returned the hat to my head and stood back to study me once more. "You did this? Yourself? All this? With Mr. Andino's money?" She nodded, pleased. "And the bellboy, Thomas? Did he ever..." She shrugged and I looked down at the floor, pained. "I guess not."

"They're waitin' on ya downstairs, Miss Ayres. Two bites of egg," she said, quickly pulling a silver fork over the plate. "Ya're gonna need yar strength."

"My pa," I said, reluctantly taking first one bite, and then the other, "used to make me poached eggs and fried eggs and soft boiled..." I took a third bite and then a fourth. "Golly, these are scrumptious," I realized.

Beatrice smiled as she lifted the fork to my mouth. She was careful not to let hollandaise sauce spill on the frock. When I finished I put the white cloth napkin to my lips and kissed it just like Mrs. Harrison had taught me.

"Are ya about ready, Miss Ayres?" Beatrice asked.

"I don't know," I said truthfully. "You want me to go downstairs and..."

"Give those newsies yarself," she offered. "That's all they really want."

I looked down at the navy blue frock and smiled. I thought about all those party lessons and napkin kisses. I recalled the many tender moments when Mrs. Harrison demonstrated the proper way to cross my ankles while seated, to remove my gloves at the table and place them in my lap, to chew with my mouth closed. But it was all the books she shared with me, not only Charlie's detective stories, the moody English novels, the poetry, but the more difficult Mr. Kipling, that she had wanted me to understand. Charlie told me that he took this book to bed, letting Mr. Kipling's melodic voice put him to sleep every night so that he would never have to finish it. I, on the other hand, couldn't put the book down. I saw Mr. Kipling's jungle as all that was wrong with New York. This, I wanted to tell Beatrice, was who I was.

I remembered the way Charlie looked at me, eyes crossed, when he offered his arm and escorted me through the hotel foyer on our way to the confectionary. I didn't know then just how heroically this New York jungle would serve me up and then spit me out. I was on my way to a candy counter with only one aim: to get out of there alive. I never imagined so many vines, so many lines.

I searched Beatrice's face. "I know you know me," I tried. Beatrice blushed. "Honestly. We've only known each other a short while and yet..." I paused. "Why is that?"

Beatrice's blush was brighter. "I don't know, Miss Ayres. Maybe it's not me. Ya're ya, ya know." She crossed the room and looked down onto the busy street below. I got the feeling she never had the chance to look down on anyone before, not from a height like this. She held her hand to her throat and paused before turning back to me. "It's comical how dolled up girls get these days." She was studying me and forming the words she was hoping to say. Before she lost her courage she said them. "We see it at Altman's all the time. An' I just, well, I just didn't think ya were silly. Or one of 'em. 'Em girls, I mean. Ya're far more sensible." She looked at me, curiously, the way Ma will sometimes look at me. "Yar bigger than ya think ya are. Brighter. Perhaps ya understand yarself. An' these girls, comin' into Altman's on their granddaddies' arms, well..." She laughed painfully.

I put my hand to my heart and looked about the room. "You have no idea how much I want to get out of here," I realized. "I was thinking maybe I could hide in a laundry cart or stow away under the table there," I said pointing, "and be taken back to the kitchen. But then what? How would I get out of there with my dignity still intact?" I laughed. "That would be just my luck to be trapped in a kitchen." Beatrice seemed to understand what I was saying and she smiled.

I turned to her and explained. "I've been trying, you know, to leave. To let go of the past. To let my pa go. To do right." She looked at me as if pondering something. "I will do right, you know."

"Now Miss Ayres, ya're scarin' me. Of course ya'll do right."

"Beatrice. I have to leave. I will." She was studying the floor, thinking. "It's time I walk out of an old story." I skipped over to her and gave her the warmest embrace. She was so alarmed she nearly fell to her knees, but when she took me by the shoulders and straightened me out she held me there for a moment and smiled.

I took her hand in mine. "I'm no longer a girl," I offered. I thought about how Mr. Andino had tossed me up on the bed, how he had pulled my thin legs into him, and how he had torn the frock lifting it over the top of my head. If I squealed I don't remember. If I cried *no* it had become all too late. "Not anymore," I added. I studied Beatrice's expression. The wheels were turning in her mind, but she said nothing. "And somehow you must have known this about me," I said, bowing slightly to her. "It's you. You know me." But Beatrice demurred.

The only thing keeping me from marching right back down to Mr. Andino's apartment and telling him what I thought of him, asking for an apology, and demanding he make things right between us was, well, me. I knew I wouldn't feel better going to him again. How could I? I turned to Beatrice, and with a hand on my heart, I explained. "I wanted any frock but the silly one I came here in, all ruffles and bows. It wasn't going to make me, me. And I so wanted..." Beatrice's eyes filled with tears. "I wanted, well, I wanted...something."

Beatrice quickly wiped away a tear that had fallen onto her plump cheek. "I will remember ya, Miss Ayres, an' this time we've had together for the rest of my life."

I stood on the tips of my toes and spun about the room letting the silk frock twirl with me. It had all the charm I loved and all the pizazz of something more. "I will remember you too," I promised. I turned to Beatrice and lowered my voice. "Why must women pretend?" I think I caught her off guard and she swallowed her words, saying something I didn't hear. But I was definitive. "There's no room for that. Not here. Not now."

Beatrice nodded, thinking. "Yes, Miss Ayres."

I scrutinized the peeling wallpaper while taking a last look at it all, stalling. "You won't tell anyone this, will you, but I think I'm beginning to understand what it takes to become a Modern. All this," I said wheezing, "is ghastly." I skipped over the fussy room to take another turn in my new shoes and sang, "The Waldorf-Astoria Hotel has just got to move with the times and redecorate in something avant-garde and chic. Like my new frock. But you didn't hear that from me."

Beatrice brightened. She crossed her hand over her heart. "I won't tell a soul."

"And you won't share..."

"Nothin', Miss Ayres. What ya've said to me...in confidence," she realized, "stays here." Her hand was on her heart as her smiling eyes shone down on me.

I apologized. "I'm not from a wealthy family."

"We know, Miss Ayres."

"I've never once been treated like this. Like royalty."

"But ya should be."

"No. No, it's terrible. Just like this room. It's nothing but a cage," I realized. Beatrice opened the door and peered down the long hallway. "I don't need it. And no one else should want me this way. It's..."

"It's all clear," said Beatrice, stepping back into the room.

I wasn't ready to leave the room. How could I? One step into the foyer and I would be found out. No one would want me then. I touched the navy silk. "It's a beautiful frock, Beatrice, and I don't want to appear ungrateful, I truly love it, but I'm taking it off the minute I get out the front door. I can't let Mr. Andino buy me this. He took..."

"Come now, Miss Ayres, no one needs to know the truth," she said, adding a touch of red lip stain to my lips. "That's only for ya."

"I don't understand."

"Ya're the most celebrated Hollywood starlet," she explained.

I turned from her and recrossed the room. "But I'm frightened. I never saw Mr. Andino as a gyp! A rake! I didn't know what he was capable of." I paused. "Of pulling me away from myself." I looked at my reflection in the mirror and realized it wasn't me, but then again it was. "Oh, Beatrice," I admitted, "Champagne killed the baby girl."

Beatrice bowed. "Of course ya're anxious, Miss Ayres. You're steppin' out in the most darin' frock. A bare leg. The smartest shoes. Forgive me," she said apologizing. "Please, forgive me. Ya're ya. An' it wasn't right of me to think otherwise."

I turned to Beatrice. "I am me. And you see it." She smiled tenderly. "But it's all just so posh I feel I should undo it," I tried.

"No ya don't," she offered. "Ya will take one look in the glass each time ya pass it by an' see yarself all new. We all will."

"But..."

"Ya're goin' places, Miss. I feel it."

I steadied my hands on the table and looked at the empty luncheon plate. "My pa," I said, willing myself not to cry, "was a good man, but he's gone." I sat in the chair and put my head down on the table.

Beatrice tiptoed clumsily over the floor and put a hand on my shoulder. "We know all about it."

I looked up at her. "You do?"

She smiled. "Your pa is lookin' down on ya. Wouldn't he want ya to..."

"...to get my due?" I asked.

I wanted her to sit down beside me, but Beatrice stood. "Your pa was a righteous man," she deemed.

"You knew him?"

"No," she said carefully, "but he helped bring ya into this world, didn't he? Ya're still his baby girl." I was truly struggling now and I swiped the back of my trembling hand over the red lip stain. "That's a mighty powerful French cosmetic," she said, eyeing me. "Has stayin' power."

"I'm angry," I hissed. "I'm so damn angry with him."

"Now, Miss Ayres, ya can't do nothin' to stop that anger, but ya can't let it stop ya from goin' downstairs." She took my hand in hers. "Ya can't stay up here forever."

I raised my head. "I know. I'm trying. But where am I going to go?"

"Oh, they'll fetch ya a car..."

"I know all about the car, Beatrice, but once I get into the car...where will it take me? I can't go home."

Beatrice was thoughtful. "I have never met anyone like ya."

"Is that good or bad?"

"Ya go forward, Miss Ayres. Like a Modern."

I stood and walked to the window. I looked for the taffy cart, but it was gone. "My pa once told me," I said, raising my hand to the glass, leaning on it, and peering down onto the street, "that no one goes forward or backwards." I shook my head. "No. We go in circles, Beatrice. And what goes around will at some other time return to you." I closed the drapes sharply. "He's not returned."

"Then go on," she tried. "Take one foot and put it..."

"I can't go backwards to the dance studio. Not dressed like this."

"Then go on back to Hollywood, Miss Ayres. Give 'em hell!"

I smiled weakly. "I need a favor, Beatrice. Just one." Beatrice stood, like a sentry, on her toes. "I don't want Mr. Andino or his car. He and I...we're nothing," I realized. "A huge mistake. I was wronged," I explained, "but I've been wronged before." I paused, thinking about my pa, his hand on the door, the per-i-lous sea he must have crossed for me. "I know girls get wronged all the time. But I can change that somehow. Can't I?"

Beatrice unveiled a pair of new white gloves from the pocket of her grey smock. "Maybe Mr. Andino did ya the greatest favor," she reasoned, handing me the expensive gloves.

"This," I choked, indicating my new frock, "a favor?"

"Ya're steppin' out, Miss Ayres. In high style."

I took the gloves from her and smiled thoughtfully. "High-steppin'."

We both took a giant leap over the thorns and sang, "Steppin' high."

I slipped my delicate hands into the soft kidskin gloves. They were far more elegant than anything Mrs. Harrison could afford. As I pulled them up to my elbows and buttoned the smooth round white pearl buttons at my wrists, I struck a pose on one of the large red roses and looked up at Beatrice. "Steppin' high at a cost," I ventured. "You know that, Beatrice. At a cost. Mr. Andino used me. He seduced me." She was quiet for a while. I wanted to know what she was thinking, but she wasn't thinking so much as she was forming words on the tip of her tongue that she wouldn't say. Or couldn't say. "He used me," I continued, "but I guess I let him." Beatrice shook her head. "I was used up by the time I met him, wasn't I? Going nowhere."

Beatrice softened. "Ya're the most celebrated. Goin' *everywhere*, Miss Ayres."

"Don't you get it, Bea?" I said affectionately. "I'm only going because of him."

She grinned. "An' me."

She was so sincere that I couldn't help but grin too. "Of course. You, and Thomas, and Tom," I added. "Mrs. H. My ma." My mind was reeling back the script. "Even Charlie." It was only a few short hours ago that I had been curled up on a settee downstairs in a sleepy hotel foyer waiting for something.

Beatrice took my impeccably clean gloved hands in her overworked ones and whispered. "I don't doubt that Railroad Tycoon got his spikes on ya. Or maybe his rivets. His draftin' pencils," she said thoughtfully, "but ya're walkin' out of here usin' him. An' me. An' the Waldorf-Astoria Hotel."

I choked. "Oh my god..."

"Usin' us to make a change for yarself," she reasoned. "Ya gotta take the bad with the good, Miss Ayres."

My eyes, searching for something, met hers. "I know this," I said painfully. "My ma. She's everyone's favorite, Bea. Everyone's. Even Hank, our butcher, says she's his champion. You see she's always demanding what she can get, the very best of what she can get from him, for her pennies like she's in there spending fins. He loves that." I was thinking of all that love in my ma and I smiled. "She goes after what she wants, Bea." I looked at her and laughed. "God better watch out when she shows up at His doorstep demanding First Class."

Beatrice laughed. It was a genuine belly laugh. "I sure am gonna miss ya, Miss Ayres."

I smiled. I was on the verge of telling her the truth, but then I thought, why? She was having fun. I was having fun. I was so hell-bent on proving Mr. Andino wrong. I wanted to go to him the hero of my own story. Didn't I? But I hadn't thought about Bea. I belonged, I guess for now, in hers. I picked up the "Social Notes" and struck a pose. "Mrs. Ogilvie has generously offered me the use of her rooms," I said, like butter melting down the sides of a stack of steaming flapjacks, "while she's away."

Beatrice swooned. "Oh, I knew it! I had my mind set on ya stayin'. I knew once ya got yar feet on our sidewalks again ya'd never wanna leave. Ya're really steppin' high now, Miss Ayres. Park Avenue. That's about as high as a girl can go."

I nodded. "I will walk," I told her, "but would you kindly bring me an umbrella? I do believe it's starting to rain."

XIII

Manhattan can be cruel. As a matter of fact, New York City, in all its modernity and pretense, is cruel to those who can't step high over the cracks in the sidewalk. I waited for Beatrice to return with an umbrella, but she never did. I waited for the rain to let up and for the street lamps to turn on before stepping through the door. I never did find out if Beatrice was sacked, but when Mr. Lucius Boomer, the hotel manager, came upstairs to bring me a box of Sherry chocolates and a vase of pink roses, compliments of the Waldorf-Astoria Hotel, I discovered that both Tom, the page, and Thomas, the bellboy, had been let go for fraternizing. I would come to suspect that Beatrice, too, had been dismissed.

I did everything in my power to help them gain reentry into their former positions, but Mr. Boomer insisted that the faults were theirs and not mine. "We have standards," he croaked, denigrating them in front of me. "And I'll see to it that you're outfitted with nothing but the best, Miss Ayres, for that is our service, but not at the expense of our reputation." He clicked his polished heels and saluted. "Our dignity."

I couldn't see it that way, but Mr. Boomer did, and no amount of persuasion moved him. I will hold them in my heart for the rest of my days, these saints who tended to me. There are ancient mythological tales told of gods and goddesses far wiser, stronger, perhaps even more agreeable, certainly more cunning, but my saints from that day were the true heroes. When I stepped out of the room I wasn't the same girl I had been the day before. I was somebody, not a nobody, but I was me. At Beatrice's urging I thanked Mr. Andino, in my mind, for the new goods. I thanked the angels in the B. Altman workroom who dyed and stitched and fabricated my new life.

I slipped past the elevator attendant and hurried down the back stairwell without another soul putting their peeping eyes on me. I simply walked past the busy reception desk, in my new hat and shoes, and ducked away from the throng of newsies in their brown suits lounging easily and most agreeably on a mish-mash of rearranged hotel furniture. I glanced at the gilded clock. It was half past nine. I imagined the men drinking club sodas and waiting an entire day for me, their Hollywood starlet, to descend. But I put my head down and continued walking right past the busy doormen, the cabbies, the bellboys, and the animated overdressed hotel guests and their stoic uncomplaining drivers. I simply walked out of the Waldorf-Astoria Hotel and into the bent heat of a Manhattan night.

The dining crowd, fashionable men and women wanting to see, and to be seen, had begun to arrive. There were unescorted flirtatious young women arriving in tea-length frocks who high-stepped their way under the arched porte cochère, having just seen the heaviest of the downpours, dragging rain-soaked hems up the stairs and through the revolving door. I stood under the covered steel-and-glass entrance in my knee-length frock and peered up into a clearing sky. "The stars will be out tonight," I thought, stepping out onto the busy sidewalk. With a practiced dance step, I leapt over one of the puddles.

I didn't know where I was going, but I knew, just as I had seen the hotel door revolving, and the misinformed women entering, that I would one day return. I skipped down the street and looked beyond the corner. My ma was hurting, of that I was certain, possibly even crying her eyes out at the thought of losing me too, but I would go to her soon, I thought, and tell her about my wilted corsage. But not tonight. Tonight I would take myself where my new shoes led me. I looked back at the hotel revelers and fought the urge to slide back into a role, to play a part, to string them all along for one more night, but I knew it wasn't something that would last. Not in a million. One photograph in the morning papers and I would be rousted from the script. I stretched my lean legs in front of me and jumped over the rain-soaked cracks in the sidewalk. If I found my way to 300 Park Avenue it probably wouldn't be an accident, although I didn't know where these legs were taking me. I only knew that I had to go. Somewhere.

When I arrived and I looked up at the imposing stone building, I counted seventeen floors. I imagined Mrs. Ogilvie at the top. I was unescorted, and although this was avant-garde and acceptable for a woman entering the Waldorf-Astoria Hotel, I knew I couldn't just waltz into Mrs. Ogilvie's life this way. I would need a plan. I lifted my head and skipped up the front steps in that high-stepping way I had perfected, somehow, in the womb of the Waldorf-Astoria. A handsome man, not handsome like Mr. Andino or Tom or Thomas, but handsome in his confidence, leapt like a gazelle up the steps beside me.

He put a gentle white-gloved hand on my elbow to help steer me through the jostling crowd. "You're somebody, aren't you?" he whispered in a foreign accent, urging me along. Together we found our way through the eager crowds as we entered one of New York City's most prestigious restaurants. "One of Mr. Sherry's confections," he explained.

If Mrs. Harrison could see me now, I thought, parting the crowd with each step. I threw my impeccably white-gloved hand to my eyes to shield them from a sudden flash of light. Everywhere I looked there were traces of a gilded life. The place screamed just how well-heeled, how influential, how respected a life here could become. I touched the brightly polished brass banister and looked directly into the camera lens. "I'm here," I realized. And I let the camera know it. I turned and looked up toward the ceiling at the pastel painted clouds parting a golden orbed sky. Cherubs fawned over one another in some romantic attempt at a heavenly dance. They wore gold wings, gold rings, and golden halos of light. "Pa," I thought, clutching the banister for all my life. "My due. Is this it?"

"Looky here, Miss," came the first shoutout. And then another. "Over here, Miss...Your eyes here, Miss." Not once did I hear them shout, "Miss Ayres." Nor did I tell them anything that would lead them to believe that I was anyone but myself. As their Autographics flashed and smoked, they called for me, hungrily.

I high-stepped alongside the dashing and agreeable man and smiled. I tried out my new voice. "Mrs. Clinton Ogilvie is expecting me."

If the newsies camped out over here with the hope of seeing someone, anyone they thought important enough to be on the inside, someone they thought could be ratcheted up a few notches in their "Social Notes," I wouldn't know. But with one mention of her name, the exotic dapper man, dressed to the nines in his black top hat, white tie, and tails, whisked me through the building. I never did find out what floor the old lady lived on, but before Mrs. Ogilvie could turn me away at her door, I curtsied and introduced myself as Miss Edith May. She welcomed the noble man, Count, as she called him, by genuflecting. Then she took me, approvingly, inside the multi-room apartment where she was eager to show off each of her six newly furbished bathrooms.

I guess I thrilled her in the Parisian-designed frock, the bobbed hair, the black pearls, and the silk hat. That cloche hat would later become all the rage. She dropped her head, ever so slightly, as if to bow, but not bow. To me.

<>

I couldn't laugh. It wasn't funny. But then again, it was, the way I would pull strings. "People do the darnedest things," I told her when we were seated in her private train car on our way to Bar Harbor, "to get themselves out of a jam. Please don't fawn over me. I'm simply a girl."

"No, my dear," cooed Mrs. Ogilvie from under her large-brimmed feathered hat. "Just look at you. You're a star."

"But you'll find me a job?" I asked, tucking my stocking feet under me as I sat uncomfortably in an overly stuffy chair. It was upholstered in a rich tapestry, a dark wine color, like the walls of the train car itself. "I came to you...um...to ask about a job. My ma, I mean my mother," I said, correcting myself, "expects me to become useful."

Her steely black eyes widened and Mrs. Ogilvie laughed deeply. The wheels on the train turned faster and I was beginning to regret my impulsiveness as we pulled away from the station. "No girl who comes to me smelling this sweet, like spun sugar," she added, "will work a day in her life."

Mrs. Ogilvie pinched a pair of wire spectacles onto the bridge of her sharp nose. She studied me and then smiled confidently. I was dressed in a traveling frock of my own choice, but I will admit it was a Mrs. Clinton Ogilvie approved emerald green number. Both the frock and the silk stockings, of the highest order, were imported from Milan and were made available to only those with the best connections. Or so she said. I wasn't unhappy with the frock. I wasn't happy. I was resigned. I knew it was the very best that her money could buy, and yet I was beginning to realize that maybe I didn't want the best. But what did I want?

I stole a glance out the little curtained window as we passed a row of dilapidated grey tenement houses. "My mother will be worried if I don't come home today."

Mrs. Ogilvie sharpened her tongue and chuckled. "Then we'll send her a telegram. It's all the rage, you know," she boasted, "being swept up like this. An unknown," she explained further, "becoming known." She pulled in her double chin and forced another haughty laugh. "You want to be someone, don't you?" she asked. I sank back into the chair and nodded uneasily. "You have the jawline, you know, to..."

"To fool people," I admitted.

"To make something of yourself," she remarked. I turned once more to look out the window as the train picked up speed. All that grey was beginning to blur. I thought about Mr. Andino. The bed. The blood between my legs. The terror I felt knowing just how bad things could be. "Edith," she said, taking my hand in hers and pumping it up and down as if to knock some sense into me. "You're going places. Just look at you."

I didn't know then just what Mrs. Ogilvie had up her elaborately embroidered ochre sleeve for me, but her "going places" and my "going places," I would soon discover, meant two different things. To her it meant climbing the social ladder to see how high a rung one could stand on, and to me, well, it meant what my pa once told me it would be. My "going places" meant that I would return to Manhattan all the wiser having taken that ride with her to Bar Harbor. I wasn't going to mill about, ill at ease, some unfinished canvas on her fog-drenched veranda sipping sherry and hoping for a sweeter taste of happiness. I am a dancer. I dance. And I feel certain that I will dance my way through this life easily putting one foot in front of the other.

<><><>

The New York Times "Social Notes"

Monday, June 19, 1922

Count Laszlo Szechenyi came on from Washington Saturday and is at the St. Regis until he leaves for Newport to join the Countess Szechenyi, who is at the Breakers with her mother, Mrs. Vanderbilt.

Mr. and Mrs. Wayland S. Townsend entertained at dinner at the Waldorf-Astoria Saturday evening for their daughter, Mrs. Thurston R. Milburn and her husband, their guests including Commander and Mrs. W. W. Galbraith, General George O. Squire, and Mr. and Mrs. William Woodward.

Tuesday, June 20, 1922

The Vice President, Calvin Coolidge, arrived at the Commodore yesterday from Washington, D. C., and will remain a few days, prior to going to Massachusetts.

Mr. Lawrence T. Andino has entertained a breakfast company Sunday morning in compliment to the film star, Miss Agnes Ayres, formerly of New York City, who will be returning shortly to her home in Hollywood Hills, California. Breakfast was served in the Palm Room.

Wednesday, June 21, 1922

Miss Mary T. Cudahy arrived on the Olympic and is at the Plaza for a few days before returning to her home, in Chicago.

Miss Edith A. May is down from Maine after a short stay in Bar Harbor with Mr. and Mrs. Clinton Ogilvie and their extended family for ten days of social dance exhibition in the ballroom, 300 Park Avenue.

Notes

CHAPTER TEN

101 *When the mind has been trained to habitual right thinking:* Mrs. Charles Harcourt, *The Blue Book of Etiquette for Women: A Guide to Conduct and Dress on All Occasions* (Philadelphia, Pennsylvania: John C. Winston, 1907), 5.

CHAPTER ELEVEN

112 *Mrs. Ogilvie will be closing her apartment tomorrow:* The New York Times "Social Notes," June 18, 1922.

THE NEW YORK TIMES "SOCIAL NOTES"

139 *Count Laszlo Szechenyi came on from Washington:* The New York Times "Social Notes," June 19, 1922.

139 *The Vice President, Calvin Coolidge:* The New York Times "Social Notes," June 20, 1922.

139 *Miss Mary T. Cudahy arrived on the Olympic:* The New York Times "Social Notes," June 21, 1922.

Books and Films

American Hotel: The Waldorf-Astoria and the Making of a Century by David Freeland

Dressed: A Century of Hollywood Costume Design by Deborah Nadoolman Landis

Last Call: The Rise and Fall of Prohibition by Daniel Okrent

Rules of Civility by Amor Towles

Save Me The Waltz by Zelda Fitzgerald

The Blue Book of Etiquette for Women: A Guide to Conduct and Dress on All Occasions by Mrs. Charles Harcourt

The New York Times "Social Notes," June 18-21, 1922

Z: A Novel of Zelda Fitzgerald by Therese Anne Fowler

The Sheik starring Rudolph Valentino and Agnes Ayres

The Story of Vernon and Irene Castle starring Fred Astaire and Ginger Rogers

Author's Note

Room Service Please originated fifteen years ago as a full-length novel. I had every intention of writing a complete novel, but each time I would revisit the manuscript over the subsequent years, Edie was adamant that she not stay cooped up in the hotel for the length of time it would take to fully develop a novel. I just couldn't do that to her. She wanted out of there. It was claustrophobic enough to leave her in the Waldorf-Astoria for an entire day, so I decided to try a different approach and embark on a journey myself—that of writing a novella. I needed to begin again and find a new way forward.

I literally tore up the previous manuscript and put myself in her shoes, figuratively speaking, and asked Edie what she wanted. I knew what I would have done in this situation. I would have asked a stranger for taxi fare and made my way back home to the Lower East Side after such a debacle of an evening. I would have returned home to what was familiar, but how long could I have stayed? I'm sure in time I would have found the courage to grieve, to let my pa go, to venture on and find my own footing, but it likely would have taken me more than a few fits and starts.

Edie is wielding her own sword. She isn't afraid to confront Mr. Andino, and this is what I love about her. But could it have been any other way? How was she going to confront that deep hole in her heart had she not gone back upstairs? Who would have helped her then? I think my sixteen-year-old self was afraid of her own shadow. I wasn't tasked with healing the holes in my heart, but I sure did know how to dig at them and puncture them repeatedly. Edie is given the opportunity to move forward and heal some of her grief. She doesn't wake up the morning after her birthday party and arrive at this awareness, but she does let herself be taken to a place of healing and acceptance. She steps unwittingly into an unknown, and with a bit of good-natured humor, starlet humor, she allows this space to open up within her. Edie gives herself a chance to explore a role, but she takes herself to her truth when she finds what does and does not fit.

Despite the arrogant game a philanderer has played, by playing her, Edie recognizes the misstep she has made. Aren't all women trapped in a kind of game? How can we play a game of checkers when we're thrown repeatedly into a game of chess? What rules apply then? In the end, Edie triumphs as a knight in her own modern armor who comes to rescue herself. Where once she superstitiously avoided thorns, this fictitious "damsel in distress" becomes aware that she now has the courage to go through them. Circumstance helps her along the way, but Edie steps into this opportunity freely and without pause.

Thank you, Edie. You've been a true friend these last fifteen years. I'm grateful I could get you out of the hotel in 137 pages and not leave you there for 300. You are an inspiration and a true Independent. You represent the early flappers whose contributions to the Jazz Age have been marginalized. Without the original suffragettes, the Mrs. Harrisons of the world, from whom you would have first learned about independence and self-respect, you might not have become as poised and dignified as I felt you needed to be to become truly Modern. From this experience, coming to know you, your self-worth and acceptance of your true nuanced self, I have come to embrace a new way of writing prose. Writing a novella has been liberating. It's like I, too, have taken off the corset and given myself permission to breathe and try on something new.

Acknowledgments

I challenge any writer to identify, accurately portray, and remember every single person who helped to influence or to support their work. My list is long and runs from birth until now. In my experience there have been people I have met along the way who saw something in me and introduced me to the ballet, theater, films, literature, art, architecture, travel, gardening, good food, wine, and lovely hotels. Not to mention philosophy, physics, and photography. Of course this would be my grandparents, and my mother and father, as it would be my many teachers and friends. This idea that we're travelers appeals to me. I write about it often. I think I have been greatly influenced by exploration of all kinds. I thank my traveling companions.

This book would not have been possible without the continued support and love of my daughters, Sarah and Lydia. They push me, whether they are aware of it or not, to continually step into the unknown. I was such a naive new mother, but with it came the opportunity to grow. I will never stop growing and looking for ways to expand this idea of "mothering" to other young women. I love this part of myself and share it eagerly.

A generous thank you to Catherine Lewis for your continued support and encouragement.

Thank you Matt Hannon for steering me in the right direction for the opening of the book and for your discerning eye on the cover design.

To Howard Means, thank you for your insights and advice.

Thank you to Linda Quennec for your understanding, insight, and delightful conversations about both *The Intrepid Meditator* and *Room Service Please.*

I am deeply grateful to J. Felice Boucher for saying yes to my request for a photograph for the book's cover. With aplomb Felice dove right in, captured the nuance I was looking for, and has brought us her vision of Edie May, a true Modern.

I am, once again, immensely grateful to Emily Kallick of Wildember Marketing for her technological know-how and can-do spirit. Without her, my manuscripts would still be buried in files on a computer and not in print in these beautiful books.

To Lee Bumsted, your unwavering sense of editing discipline and know-how is bewildering, to say the least. How do you see what you see? Without you, what a mess I would be.

Thank you to my Naropa University family of teachers and friends who have helped me trust the experimental writer in me waiting to emerge. I found you at the right time in my life.

You are here, on these pages and in my heart, even if I have not singled you out by name. You have held me when I was hurt, lifted me when I was down, and given me security and warmth. I know that you are there for me, my loved ones, colleagues, and friends. May we continue to share this sweet time together. I find that I am so inspired by the smallest of things. Know that if you have said it, felt it, or dreamt it, and I have been witness, I will find a way to honor you in my work. I can't help it. I am always looking and listening.

Author Interview

With Dr. Linda Quennec, author of *Fishing for Birds*

1. In the beginning, Edie talks about "what might have been the most unrehearsed night of my life." How does the idea of a life (or moments in a life) lived without rehearsal resonate with you? In what ways does this idea of throwing away the script connect to your explorations in *The Intrepid Meditator*?

I very much dislike living without a script, but I am learning to adopt this way of being. Before I graduated from college and got married, where up to that point everything in my life had fallen into a kind of line, I never knew how discombobulating life would become. I thought things played out in a linear fashion. First this, then that. Expect this, receive that. When suddenly nothing appeared as I thought it should or had, and my life was no longer falling into place following some "script," I felt as though I had been left on life's stage with one unrehearsed moment coming quickly after the other. I wanted to write about this to put words to expectation and what happens when these expectations, our scripts, might need to be reevaluated and rewritten.

I grew up with the stage as a metaphor and a platform for my life. I studied theater, and both my grandmothers and my mother were stage actors and directors in our local community. I was taught at a very young age the power of telling a story through movement and motivation. In *The*

Intrepid Meditator, I invite the reader to tear up their own script and rewrite for themselves an opportunity to go to their authentic truth. Edie is the invitation personified as a character on a stage set. She is misidentified as a screen actress, put into a delicate situation where she can either reinvent herself and go with the experience, as it leads her along in an unrehearsed manner, or return to her incomplete unexplored self. I wanted Edie to be clever, a true Modern, and to be able to self-identify that she is not what people expect her to be. I wanted her to serve as a smart, self-aware role model for today's young women. The irony, if you can call it this, is I thought it would be fun to write the novella as a kind of screenplay, taking the reader into a script to then ultimately ask them to witness the tearing up, and then the rewriting of it.

2. The morning after Edie's initially intoxicating evening on the ballroom floor with Mr. Andino, which ended up taking a dark turn, there is a moment when she tells Tom that she contemplated leaving the Waldorf-Astoria. This felt like a sort of "sliding doors" moment for her, and the prologue suggests this as well. What was happening in that moment that made her decide to stay? What might have happened to her if she had chosen otherwise? What gave her the confidence to consider confronting a man who was essentially a predator?

The revolving, opening, or sliding door is a metaphor for opportunity, for change, for experience, for outcome. We encounter many "sliding doors" moments throughout our lives, I'm certain of it, one after the other. Are these premeditated or do they just happen? More times than not, I think they are spontaneous. We have these moments where we go one way, and had we gone the other, or made a different decision, our lives would have been different. We are left going through these experiences unaware of the different consequences and outcomes. But why then do we seem to come back around? Can these doors take us through one experience and then lead us back to a previous starting point?

What would have happened to Edie had she gone home? We'll never know, because as much as we might think she had the confidence to stay and confront Mr. Andino, it was ultimately the motion of being caught up in something she couldn't get out of, like a revolving door, that kept her from leaving. And this sets off a series of events that forces Edie to peel back what lies broken inside of her. Was this anger, hurt, betrayal? Is she compelled to stay, not because she has confidence, but because she is still searching for her father, driven by something she has not yet identified?

3. To tell Edie's story, you use the device of breaking the fourth wall. What inspired this decision?

Women are compromised and all too often taken advantage of intellectually, physically, and psychologically. By using the technique of breaking the fourth wall, I wanted to give Edie an opportunity to become a teacher and a friend. I would give her the stage where she could invite other young women, by addressing them, intimately, to share this moment with her. I wanted Edie and the reader to have an opportunity to form a bond, a level of trust so that they could be there for one another. Perhaps together they would be able to acknowledge the very difficult disenfranchised moments most women will at some point find themselves in. Before we can right wrongs I feel we must right ourselves so that we become stronger, more knowledgeable, and trusting.

Had I delved deeper into the trauma of rape or psychological wrong-doing, this would have been a very different story. *Room Service Please* is deliberately not that story. But nor did I want to be flippant about a woman wronged. I see Edie's vulnerability as a teaching tool. It is through intimacy that Edie shares her experience. I wanted to ask the question: can a woman make a change for herself by seeing one small thread (clothing and stitches and threads are important metaphors in the story) of positivity in a hurtful situation? Would she be able to flip her own narrative and find a more productive, creative, opportunistic solution to lift her up after she has been wronged? Why fall victim again and again? When and how can women begin to shift rather than continue to let others, not just men, but others, direct their feelings? By breaking the fourth wall, I felt that I could more intimately share Edie's inner world and invite the reader to explore their own.

4. New York City is described as "sleepy" in the sense that "no one has a mind of their own." What does this mean to you, in reference to the timeframe of the novella? How does this relate to our current cultural climate?

That particular line changed multiple times. I had a hard time conveying, in a single sentence, the essence of the novella. I needed one sentence to put the reader on this path and I had no idea how I was going to do it! By putting Edie in a hotel where people sleep, make love, drink, dance, sing, play, create, dream, plan treaties, counsel, bargain, serve, are served, move through revolving doors, and go up and down elevators, this reinforced the idea that we are all surrounded by mechanisms, machines, and movement. Edie is misidentified as a starlet and whisked up into this motion, tipping her out of balance for a bit, yet making her anything but sleepy. She is physically and intellectually in motion, curious and compelled to learn and grow.

The novella takes place in 1922 on the cusp of a cultural awakening when young women were beginning to cut their hair, shorten their hemlines, and break free of societal expectations, the metaphorical corset. The Roaring Twenties were about the dawning of a phenomenon that I think young women today feel expected to adhere to: dance, play, sing, party, flirt, repeat. But young women are also very smart and intellectually empowered. It is on us to help them see themselves this way.

Our social media platforms are disastrous at conveying nuance. I would like to scoop impressionable young women up into my arms and invite them not to get caught up in the moving social media machine, but to take their own steps in life by recognizing nuance, characterization, plot points, and clichés. It is my hope that women will wake up, become a part of the self-empowerment movement, and begin to make changes from inside this machine instead of retreating and allowing the motion to swallow them up. I deliberately set the novella one hundred years in the past so that I could circle, a big theme in the book, the past around to make it relevant to today.

5. The characters Tom, Thomas, and Beatrice all seem, in their own ways, to open portals to deeper emotional experiences for Edie.

How do these moments of connection bring her to an eventual point of courage, and the ability to walk away from her scripted life?

We don't walk through life alone, and I feel it is on us to learn to appreciate those who travel alongside us. We will travel with loved ones and we will bump up against people who deliberately challenge us. As difficult as this is for us to accept, I am certain they all belong. Tom, Thomas, Beatrice, and even Mr. Andino, act, in their own ways, as catalysts for change. Through each of these encounters, I see Edie walking first through a physical shift, then a psychological shift, and then toward a place where she will come to accept this shift. To further demonstrate who she is, and how she sees herself, I wanted each of these characters to become her "dance partners." What Edie has lost, she gains by dancing alongside them toward greater self-awareness.

In the small space of a novella, I didn't give myself, or Edie, or the reader a lot of time to experience the motion, or should I say this notion, of change. Rather than have these changes happen over the course of a full-length novel, I humorously liked to think I could use the revolving door as an image for change. Imagine coming in through the door in one costume and circling out the same door hours later as a whole new you. I hope the reader will entertain this simplistic approach and not take me to task for pushing Edie through this change too quickly. Use this story as an example, an extension of what you will find in *The Intrepid Meditator*. And by all means, I hope you will answer this question for yourself.

6. Edie is a powerful and courageous young woman. How did this character come to you?

Edie is the me I want to be. She is the me I am becoming. She is my Truth. She is inside each of us, tucked away and waiting to be discovered. She is, in my mind, Grace personified. And it was Mary Magdalene who inspired me. Not the Christian personification, per se, because I see her much more fully than a contemporary religious figure. Rather, she is the light in a moment of darkness.

7. I have so enjoyed this novella, as well as *The Intrepid Meditator*, and the way they are in conversation with one another. Can you tell us what you have coming up next?

Room Service Please is the culmination of my free online meditation series and *The Intrepid Meditator* conceptualized as fiction. I plan on repeating this same sequence starting in February 2023. I will offer a one-year subscription for a series of more advanced meditations, a companion book entitled *Hidden Voices and Our Parallel Lives*, and another coming-of-age novella.

Taking place over the course of one day, *The Longest Day* tells the story of sixteen-year-old Ellen Abigail Allen, who attends a Washington D.C. charter school. The Craftsman School was hastily put together at the start of the Covid-19 pandemic in 2020 when Ellen was in the fourth grade. It is prestigious and designed for serious students, but five years later, as the world continues to navigate the effects of this ongoing pandemic, the school has become a tomb of expectation and competition. Ellen is accused of cheating. What happens next unearths one of the more mysterious unexplored theories surrounding the Egyptian Queen Nefertiti and her monotheistic reign.

I look forward to continuing this journey with you!

aliciacahalanelewis.com